It No Long...
What...
Held Th...

She didn't care anymore. It didn't matter how different their opinions were, or how hard it was to understand him. She wanted him to keep his hands on her; she wanted him to keep on caressing her; she wanted his kiss. That was all she wanted in the whole world.

"Tracey," he murmured against her mouth, "this is what I wanted to do the other night." His voice was low and rough with desire. "This is what I've wanted to do ever since the first minute I saw you."

His eyelids were heavy with desire as slowly, thoroughly, he began to kiss her.

GENA DALTON
is a wife and mother as well as a writer, but her interests don't stop there. She is fascinated by Ozark-Appalachian folk culture, does tole painting, gardens, and is interested in horses.

Dear Reader:

Romance readers have been enthusiastic about the Silhouette Special Editions for years. And that's not by accident: Special Editions were the first of their kind and continue to feature realistic stories with heightened romantic tension.

The longer stories, sophisticated style, greater sensual detail and variety that made Special Editions popular are the same elements that will make you want to read book after book.

We hope that you enjoy this Special Edition today, and will enjoy many more.

Please write to:

Jane Nicholls
Silhouette Books
PO Box 236
Thornton Road
Croydon
Surrey CR9 3RU

GENA DALTON
Wild Passions

Silhouette Special Edition
Originally Published by Silhouette Books
division of
Harlequin Enterprises Ltd.

First published in Great Britain 1985 by Mills & Boon Ltd, 15–16 Brook's Mews, London W1A 1DR

© Gena Dalton 1984

Silhouette, Silhouette Special and Colophon are Trade Marks of Harlequin Enterprises B.V.

ISBN 0 373 48638 3

23-0485

Made and printed in Great Britain by Richard Clay (The Chaucer Press) Ltd, Bungay, Suffolk

For Luke and for Gary,
with thanks.

Other Silhouette Books by Gena Dalton

Silhouette Special Edition

Sorrel Sunset
April Encounter

*For further information about
Silhouette Books please write to:*

Jane Nicholls
Silhouette Books
PO Box 236
Thornton Road
Croydon
Surrey CR9 3RU

Wild Passions

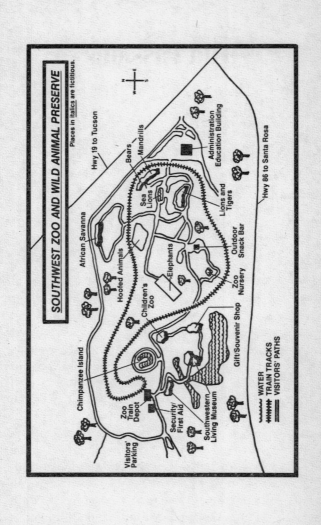

SOUTHWEST ZOO AND WILD ANIMAL PRESERVE

Places in italics are fictitious.

N
W · E
S

Hwy 19 to Tucson

Hwy 86 to Santa Rosa

Bears

Mandrills

Administration
Education Building

Sea
Lions

Lions and
Tigers

African Savanna

Outdoor
Snack Bar

Hoofed Animals

Elephants

Children's
Zoo

Zoo
Nursery

Chimpanzee Island

Zoo
Train
Depot

Gift/Souvenir Shop

Security/
First Aid

Southwestern
Living Museum

Visitors'
Parking

〜〜〜〜 WATER
✕✕✕✕ TRAIN TRACKS
━━━━ VISITORS' PATHS

Chapter One

Tracey drove the pickup over the last little incline at the same rapid rate she had used all the way from her office. Visions of a wild rhino frightening cattle and trampling fences had glued her foot to the accelerator, and when she finally stepped on the brake the vehicle slid to a stop in a spray of gravel and sand. She got out quickly to walk toward several zoo employees who were talking with some men on horseback near the animal preserve's larger truck and a Jeep.

"Ms. Johnston, I'm sure sorry," one of her employees called, coming to meet her. "Somethin' went wrong with the winch, and it dropped the crate, rhino and all. It fell three or four feet. When it broke open he got all excited and ran around some, and then he trotted right back out the gate the truck had just come through."

Tracey nodded, assimilating the details of the morning's disaster. "It wasn't your fault, Mac. At least Maqu wasn't hurt or killed." She hoped that she sounded more composed than she felt.

Mac's creased, worried face broke into a smile. "Right. Then we would've *really* had trouble."

She tried to smile back. The rhino could *still* be hurt or killed. That was another major worry that had tormented her since she'd heard that he'd escaped.

The litany of awful possibilities that had begun with that phone call kept going around in her head as Mac led her over to join the others, and it pushed their greetings and conversation into the back of her mind.

She shaded her eyes with her hand and looked around for a glimpse of the enormous creature.

"He disappeared over that way," Mac's partner told her, waving one hand toward the west. "It's been five minutes or so since we seen him."

Mac chimed in, trying to comfort her, "I don't think he's gone far. We'll get him as soon as Doc Reed comes."

She didn't answer. She just kept looking in the direction the men had pointed, listening to their comments with half an ear. Her stomach was tied into one enormous knot, and it wouldn't unwind until that white rhino was safely in his enclosure at his new home.

Something moved in the distance, and she started, but it wasn't Maqu.

It was a man on horseback, coming over the horizon toward them in the hard glare of the sun. The two of them seemed to move over the earth as one being; the clean lines of the man's broad shoulders and lean hips moving in silent concert with the palomino he rode drew her gaze and held it.

"It's okay, boys, just stay downwind of him. He's headed into that arroyo now," the cowboy shouted. Authority vibrated in his deep voice as he called to them again. "Jim, be sure the Jeep's ready. When Dr. Reed gets here I'll use it to drive him out to dart the rhino."

He was near enough now for her to see the strongly formed angles of his face, its features shadowed by the brim of his Western hat.

"And Hawk, you ride over there to the rim of the arroyo and keep an eye on the animal in case he decides to run some more."

He noticed Tracey then. He gathered the worn leather reins at his hip with one hand and came to a stop only a few feet from her, reaching up with his other hand to push the hat back from his forehead. His long form relaxed in the saddle.

"Hello." His glance flicked from her to the logo on her truck that announced "Southwest Zoo and Wild Animal Preserve" and back again. "You come out to join in the excitement? Could be dangerous, you know."

"I came out to help recapture the rhino," she retorted stiffly, stung by the lightness in his tone.

His keen eyes took in every detail of her, moving from her windblown hair to her finely boned face and then over the generous curves of her figure, revealed by the strong breeze and her clinging ecru silk blouse.

They lingered appreciatively for a moment, then moved over her copper-colored linen skirt and down her long legs to her neat businesslike pumps.

Suddenly she was aware that the words she'd just spoken were totally incongruous with her appearance. She wanted to say something that would establish her authority as acting director of the zoo and animal preserve, to tell him that she'd dressed that morning for a meeting with some visitors from the Brookfield Zoo and not for a rhinoceros chase across the desert.

Her lips parted, but somehow she couldn't organize any of the concepts in her mind into sentences. His eyes were blue. A deep, shimmering blue that reflected the Arizona sky overhead.

His lips curved into a slow smile under the tawny thickness of his mustache.

"Well, now, I believe that's all pretty well under control," he drawled. "Dr. Reed is on his way, and so is the forklift, so it shouldn't be too long before this famous rhino is right back in his new home."

The palomino was restless, and it pulled a little at the bit and danced sideways, its hooves scraping against the rocky ground. The muscles in the cowboy's thighs moved under his tight, faded jeans as he gripped the horse's sides, but he made no other response to its nervousness.

He sat the horse the same way he talked, she thought, with a confidence that bordered on arrogance. As if he were in charge of the whole world and had it well in hand.

"I know all about the arrangements," she answered

dryly. "I'm the one who made them. I'm Tracey Johnston, assistant administrator at Southwest."

He raised one sandy-colored eyebrow in surprise. "I've been wanting to meet you," he replied. "I'm Davis Turnbo."

Shock raced through her. Davis Turnbo! She'd assumed that this dusty, sweaty cowboy with the air of authority was the foreman on the Turnbo ranch. How could he be the man she'd been hearing about ever since she'd arrived at Southwest?

That Davis Turnbo was the chairman of the board of directors at Southwest and one of the wealthiest, most influential ranchers and businessmen in Arizona. He was the founder of the zoo and animal preserve; this whole institution that she was coming to love had been his idea. He had fought in the legislatures of four states for the necessary funding.

This Davis Turnbo was entirely different from the older, sedate businessman she had imagined.

In one smooth motion he dismounted and came around the horse to her, handing the reins to one of his cowboys. He removed the hat completely, and as he came nearer she saw that he did indeed look as if he had sprung from the earth itself. Up close his eyes were even bluer than the sky, and his hair and his mustache were streaked like the sand with dozens of shades of blond and tan and gold, some of the strands almost white from long hours in the sun. His forehead was creased and sweaty from the band of the hat.

She held out her hand as he approached, and he took it into his large hard one.

"I've intended to drop by your office and welcome you to Southwest, but I haven't quite made it. How's your job going?"

"Who can tell?" she answered with a rueful smile. "Right now I just can't believe that we lost a white rhino. Isn't it enough that Gerald has been in the hospital with hepatitis and I've had to take responsibility for everything?"

He smiled back, with his lips and with his eyes, and she wasn't sure she had the strength to take her hand back again. "Don't worry about it. In a couple of hours we'll have this animal all settled in his new enclosure. We have to get him on display after the way we've been playing up his arrival. You know we can't keep his public waiting!"

He was so calm, so sure that they'd recapture Maqu with no trouble, that the tension in her stomach eased just a little.

The noise of a car drifted to them, and they turned to see another of the zoo's dark green vehicles approaching. A huge yellow forklift followed it at a distance.

"See, what did I tell you? Here's the doctor now."

Dr. Reed drove up to them with a flourish and stepped out, crisply neat in his khaki work uniform.

"All right, where is he?" he asked in his lilting Canadian accent. "We've worked a long time getting this rhino's quarters ready, and I intend for him to show a little appreciation instead of turning up the horn on his nose and running away."

Tracey was able to laugh a little. "So do I. We can't let him get away with being so ungrateful."

"He's over there exploring an arroyo," Davis answered, gesturing toward the distant figures of Hawk and his horse. "I'll drive you in the Jeep."

Dr. Reed nodded briskly and was turning to take the capture gun from his truck when they heard an indistinguishable shout. Hawk was galloping toward them, the strangely graceful figure of the rhino moving in the distance behind him.

"Good, he's out in the open!" the veterinarian exclaimed. "But I think he's completely terrified your cowboy."

"He'll get over it," Davis replied with a laugh, already running toward the Jeep. He turned and called back over his shoulder, "Tracey, set up some spotters in case he changes direction and decides to really take off."

Dr. Reed, the lethal-looking capture gun in his hand, ran to join Davis, and Tracey dispatched the men on horseback to vantage points in different directions. Then she sent Mac in her small truck to try to keep the rhino going on a relatively straight course for the Jeep's approach.

That turned out not to be necessary; Maqu kept running in an almost straight line, plunging around and over the cacti and clumps of desert brush and grasses. Davis drove the Jeep into a position that was parallel to the animal's course and skillfully kept the vehicle a consistent distance away from the enormous rhino as he ran.

Tracey watched from the cab of Mac's truck, fascinated as always by the practically prehistoric animal.

His tail was over his back, and his head, with its curving horn, was lowered until it almost touched the ground. For a second she forgot her tension as she marveled at the speed with which he ran; it was incredible that such an enormous, awkward-looking animal could be so fast.

Finally Maqu angled to a spot fifty yards or so away from her. He was so close that she could hear the sound he made, almost like a barrel of water being shaken, and she could see his heavy wrinkles and the streaks of sweat that darkened his gray skin.

Davis kept the Jeep in position, and Dr. Reed leaned out of the vehicle and leveled the capture gun. He made a solid hit; the dart pierced the animal's shoulder with an audible "clunk."

Unconsciously she breathed a little prayer that he would be all right. Every animal was an individual, and there was a possibility that Maqu wouldn't be able to tolerate the standard dosage of the tranquilizer.

The rhino galloped forward about a hundred feet, then stopped and turned to face them. Dr. Reed held up his hand, and Davis stopped the vehicle.

Maqu stood very still and stared at it for what seemed to Tracey to be an eon, then he shook his head and slowly started to move his legs. He began picking up speed every second and finally, his head lowered, he charged the Jeep.

Tracey gripped the truck's steering wheel, unable to breathe. The beast seemed twice the size of his target, and Dr. Reed and Davis looked frighteningly unprotected. Terror washed through her, and she wanted to close her eyes, but somehow she couldn't.

Then it was over. The drug took effect, and Maqu collapsed gently onto his stomach only a few feet away from the Jeep.

Davis and Dr. Reed got out and went toward him. As soon as her hands had stopped shaking and the strength had returned to her legs Tracey left the truck and ran to them.

Dr. Reed was already checking the rhino. "His breathing seems to be okay, but we don't want to leave him unconscious too long. Let's get the forklift and the big truck over here."

The other men were all drifting toward the spot where the rhino had gone down, and Tracey called to Mac to bring the truck.

As soon as she had finished giving him instructions, her eyes went to Davis, almost of their own volition. He was talking with the forklift operator, but he felt the brief look and turned to smile at her. Then he dismissed the man and began walking toward her.

His eyes were still bright with exhilaration from the chase, and an elemental excitement seemed to be vibrating within him. His whole body radiated tension. His grin flashed at her, triumphant.

Her breathing hadn't quite steadied yet; the frightening charge was so fresh in her mind that she hadn't truly absorbed the fact that the rhino had been caught.

"For a minute there I thought Maqu was going to do you in," she said, her voice shaking a little.

"So did I," he answered. "I expected him to fall right where he stopped, and when he didn't I thought he was going to steamroll right over us." He chuckled, and his even teeth gleamed at her from beneath the sandy-colored mustache. "It's a good thing we'll only have one of these cantankerous things; I don't believe Southwest is ready to cope with two."

She felt herself begin to relax. It was over. They'd recaptured Maqu before he'd done any damage, and none of the disasters she'd been imagining was going to happen.

She chuckled. "Well, we'll have to get ready, because I'm planning to get another one very soon. I just hope we get the winch fixed before then. I don't think my nerves could take having to go through all this again."

"Oh, we'll never get another one that soon," he said casually, still looking down into her eyes. Without waiting for her reaction he looked away, squinting into the sun to watch the men trying to load the rhino onto the truck.

"But we have to!" she protested. "We have to get our breeding program started so the preserve can be built up. It takes a long time to create a really good one."

His eyes flashed back to hers. "We can't. The legislatures will cut their appropriations in half three years from now, and we have to develop the display zoo before then. It'll be our money-maker."

His matter-of-fact voice was terrifying as well as

infuriating. It held a tone of certainty that said that his pronouncement was an unchangeable truth.

"But we can't make Southwest nothing but a display zoo! That's a betrayal of the whole spirit in which it was founded."

"I know all about the spirit in which it was founded," he replied, glancing at her quickly before returning his attention to Maqu. "I'm the one who founded it. I went to the legislatures of four states and browbeat them into giving us funds. I traveled around speaking to civic groups until I can never eat another bite of creamed chicken. I—"

"I know you're the founding father," she said sarcastically, "but that doesn't mean that you have the training—or the right—to direct the whole institution."

Two spots of dark red appeared on his high cheekbones. She had his full attention now.

"I don't have to have a college degree in zoo administration to figure out that if the display zoo isn't given priority, this institution can*not* become even partially self-supporting," he told her firmly, his eyes very dark, deeply blue. "Maqu's going to be a great drawing card to get visitors to the zoo this summer, and I'm glad we have him, but white rhinos are expensive to acquire. We can't buy another one for a long time."

He pulled his hat down on his forehead and turned again to watch the driver of the forklift moving into position. His gesture said that the subject was closed.

A chill washed over her in spite of the desert heat. "That very attitude just proves how little you know about the whole business," she burst out. In a second she forgot about everything except her work, the passion to save animals, which was practically her life. Words came pouring from her before she even knew what she was going to say.

"You sound like someone who directed a zoo twenty-five years ago! Don't you know that now it's considered immoral to keep an animal caged up alone? People are waking up, Davis! We're finally realizing that we do the animals *and* ourselves an injustice unless we give them some approximation of their natural habitats and some of their own kind to live with!"

She spoke so fervently that his anger faded. He tried to listen to her, but suddenly the only one of his senses that worked was his sight. He couldn't hear or feel or smell or taste, because he couldn't get enough of looking at her.

At her eyes. They were wide and full of lights, their color nearly impossible to name. They'd be called hazel, he supposed, but that was a poor word to describe their tawny richness beneath her thick black lashes.

But it wasn't their color, it was that intensity she had that made them blaze. She was a passionate woman.

The thought moved his gaze from her eyes to her full mouth. An almost irresistible urge to kiss her swelled in him.

"And it's the only way to save them. We have to recreate the right conditions so that they'll breed in captivity Davis, every day that passes puts many species a step closer to extinction. We have to develop our preserve right now so we can bring some of the threatened ones here."

She pushed back the heavy strands of hair that were blowing against her face, and it seemed strange to watch her do it. He felt that somehow it should have been his hand that did that.

Involuntarily he leaned toward her, searching vaguely for the thread of the conversation.

"Sort of a Noah's Ark, right?"

"Yes," she agreed enthusiastically.

"Well, unlike Noah, we have to buy our animals and provide habitats for them."

"And we can do it if we really try to find a way."

"You won't find it without money."

"But money is secondary in this, don't you see?" she explained to him eagerly. "Modern zoos and preserves have an obligation to put preservation and breeding first."

His blue eyes were opaque; they told her nothing. "Money can't be secondary," he said flatly. "The preserve has to be on solid financial ground."

"Exactly. But it's just a matter of setting priorities. We can figure out how to use the funds we already have in order to do a little bit of everything."

He chuckled a little and shook his head sadly, as if she were the most naive person he'd ever met.

"Look, Tracey, the money we have coming in over the next few months is earmarked for other things."

"Well, let's un-earmark it! Let's change the budget

and get this preserve on its way to becoming one of the best in the country. We have to remember our purpose."

Her zealous tone made him smile. "It's impossible now. Everything is set for the next year. Come to the board meeting tomorrow night and go over the budget with us and you'll see that it's true. Then, if you can find the money to buy more rhinos or more margays or more Arabian oryx or perhaps some elephants from Sri Lanka, you can have it. I'm telling you, it just isn't there."

That same implacable tone was there again, and it made her furious. *Why* couldn't he understand? If he knew as much as he seemed to about the species he'd just named, he ought to realize that someone needed to take action now to prevent their extinction!

A shout went up, and they turned to see that the forklift was in place under the big rhino. At Dr. Reed's signal the operator lifted the heavy animal up, then up a little higher, and moved it over to hover above the bed of the big truck that Mac had driven into place. Then, slowly, the operator dropped the machinery lower and lower to deposit the huge body.

"Okay, let's go," the veterinarian shouted. "We can't leave him on his side any longer than we absolutely have to." He jumped into the passenger seat of the truck, and Mac gunned the motor, freeing the wheels from the sand. He waved at Tracey as they passed, building speed for a quick trip back to the preserve.

She turned back to Davis. "I have to go now; I want

to be there when Dr. Reed gives the antidote and they unload Maqu. But I'm not giving up about these acquisitions. I had no idea when I came here that the main thrust would be toward the zoo."

"It is, but only temporarily," he answered. "Only for these first three years. Come to the board meeting, and I think you'll see the whole picture much more clearly."

"But three years is so long . . ." she began; then she stopped. She didn't have time to argue with him now.

Her jaw tightened stubbornly. "I'm going to take you up on that invitation," she said. "We can talk then. It's nice to have met you, Davis."

"I enjoyed meeting you, Tracey," he drawled. "And I'm looking forward to seeing you tomorrow night."

Her mind was already whirling with plans as she turned back to her truck. Gerald was her ally, and he'd be at the board meeting, too. He was just as eager as she was to develop the preserve, so he could help her present her case. She'd bring in documentation about the species that were living every day in danger, and after she'd explained her point of view and Gerald had backed her up, surely the rest of the board would find money someplace—at least for more rhinos.

But why couldn't Davis see the need, too? Why did he have to be so hard and unyielding?

She stopped for a moment and turned back, on impulse wanting to try again, but when she looked at him, she didn't speak. He was standing still, completely remote, his features a bronzed mask. He really *was* a part of the earth, she thought. Probably he had been formed from one of the sandstone cliffs that loomed in the distance.

He watched her walk toward the pickup truck, the supple skirt clinging to her shapely thighs in the breeze. Her dark bronze-colored hair shot sparks from the sun, absorbing its heat and giving it back again, and he moved his hand restlessly as if he had touched its fire and it had burned him.

She climbed into the truck, starting the motor almost before she'd closed the door, and he stood, the heels of his boots dug into the earth, until she'd driven out of sight. The last glimpse he had of her was the line of her profile, pure and white against the blue of the sky.

Jim's voice broke into his thoughts. "Good-lookin' woman, huh, boss? Don't see many like that around this place."

Without answering Davis reached for the reins that the cowboy was holding and swung into the saddle.

It was more than that, he admitted to himself as he pointed the big palomino toward the house. She was good looking, but there was something else, besides. There was something about her that spoke to him deep inside. Something that called to a part of him that had lain dormant for so long that he'd thought it was dead.

Well, it needed to stay dead, he muttered, his gut twisting with painful memories for the first time in months. Five years ago in an agony of loss and guilt he'd decided never again to let a woman touch him deeply, and nothing was going to alter that.

Anything that aroused the longing that things could be any different was just like the staghorn cactus that dotted his ranch in the spring. Its flowers were open and beautiful, but it was something you'd better not touch. Its thorns could rip you apart.

Chapter Two

Tracey shifted her attaché case so she could push open the heavy glass doors, then walked briskly across the lobby of Southwest's administration building. She didn't take time as she usually did to stop and say good-morning to the prairie dog in the cage just outside the education curator's office, or to watch the fish who lived in the aquarium beside him. Instead she went directly into the reception area that separated her office from that of her boss, Gerald Nelson.

Lottie, the secretary they shared, looked up from her typewriter with her usual smile. "Good morning, Tracey. You're in early today."

"Yes. I thought that maybe if I came in early and stayed late, I could get this place under control."

"Well, I don't know," Lottie answered. "You may have to stay around the clock to accomplish that. I'll tell you why as soon as you put down your things and get settled. You have to be sitting down for this news."

A small cold hand clutched at Tracey's stomach. Some other enormous problem was all she needed to compound the one she already had. She'd spent half the night studying the budget that Davis had talked so much about, determined to prove him wrong, but the effort had been terribly depressing. One look at all those numbers had told her that they hadn't been written with the preserve in mind.

She forced her thoughts back to the present and searched the secretary's narrow face. "Okay, Lottie, let's have it. Do we have another escapee? Has someone run away before breakfast?"

"No, no, nothing like that," the older woman reassured her. "As far as I know every single animal is present and accounted for."

"Well, then," Tracey said firmly, "come right in here and explain that remark to me."

She went into her office, and by the time she'd slipped out of her loose jacket and put the attaché case on her desk, Lottie was coming in with a steaming mug of coffee for her. "Drink this while you listen," the secretary urged. "It'll fortify you."

"Lottie, please," Tracey said, taking the cup and sitting down at her desk. "What's going on?"

"It's Gerald," Lottie replied as she slid into the leather armchair across from Tracey. "He called a few minutes ago to say that he still won't be coming back to work for a while."

Tracey's hand stopped midway to her mouth. "Poor

Gerald! I had no idea it was that serious. Will he be in the hospital long?"

"For a week or so. But even after he's home he's to have bed rest and no visitors."

"So we can't go see him. Will you order some flowers, Lottie?"

"I'll do it first thing. Now, do you . . ."

Then the full implication of the news struck Tracey. "Oh, no!" she breathed. "I've hardly learned my own job and now I'll have to do his, too!"

"You can do it," Lottie assured her. "You've at least talked to him about almost everything in the few months you've been here."

Tracey nodded absently, her brain racing. "About almost everything except the budget," she murmured. It had been written by Gerald with the advice of the board members. "And that's what I need to know the most about right now."

She felt the pressure that had been bearing down on her yesterday during Maqu's escape and all through the anxious night that had followed begin to intensify. It spread its tendrils and made her hand tremble a little as she set the coffee cup onto the desktop. Any other time she might have loved the challenge of directing all of Southwest by herself, but right now she didn't want to be alone. She desperately needed an ally if she was going to begin to fight for immediate funding for the preserve.

The long hours she'd spent over the computer print-outs flashed through her mind again. The budget was set up so that almost all of the legislative grants for the next year would go for the development of the display zoo. She'd need all the help she could get to pry loose any of the amounts in those neat columns to use to buy animals for the breeding preserve.

She would also need all the help she could get to deal with Davis Turnbo. His blue eyes had haunted her dreams and come between her and the budget printout more than once last night.

She shook her head as the image threatened to return, and wrapped both hands around the warm cup. "But poor Gerald!" she exclaimed, her thoughts going back to her boss. "How long will it be before he can come back to work?"

"He isn't sure. You're to call him this afternoon for details."

Tracey nodded and ran a hand through her thick hair. "Well, then, Lottie, it looks as if we're on our own for a few days, at least," she said in what she hoped was an entirely confident tone. "We'd better get busy."

They talked about her schedule for the day and combined her appointments and duties with the most urgent ones on Gerald's agenda; then they tried to find slots later in the week for the less important ones. After Lottie had gone to make the necessary phone calls Tracey dictated a couple of memos into her recorder, but all the time one level of her mind was concentrating on the meeting scheduled for that night. If there was any way to convince the board to vote against that budget, she would have to find it before seven-thirty that evening.

As soon as she managed to find a little free time, she

called Gerald, hoping that she could find a way to mention the problem to him and maybe get his advice on how to handle it. He sounded tired, however, and she couldn't bring herself to tell him that she was going to do something as bold as present a challenge to the budget. He merely gave her a few instructions, and then they talked in generalities about the meeting that evening. After that he hung up, exhausted.

Tracey tried and tried all day to make some time to go over the figures again, but it was almost five o'clock that afternoon before she had the chance. She stayed at her desk long past the time she usually left, past Lottie's departure, studying the long green-and-white sheets, looking for nonessentials that could be eliminated.

Finally she glanced at the slim gold watch on her wrist. Six-thirty! The meeting was set to begin in an hour, and she still had to shower and change. She had to look her very best so that she would have the confidence to take on the entire board of directors.

And because she'd be seeing Davis Turnbo again, a small voice inside her suggested.

With a sigh she folded the perforated sheets and slid them into her case. There was nothing in particular that she could fight to have eliminated. She would simply have to make an appeal on philosophical grounds. She would explain the concept of the zoo as a kind of Noah's Ark, as Davis had put it, and she would be so convincing that the board would find her some money from *someplace*. Surely they had at least enough money for one or two more white rhinos to keep Maqu company and begin a breeding program for that one endangered species.

As soon as she got home she hurriedly fed her horses and her dog; then she showered and washed her hair, setting it on hot curlers while she applied her makeup.

She brushed her hair into loose waves that swirled around her face, and went to her closet to choose just the right outfit to wear. She wanted to look very professional and businesslike.

And feminine and beautiful, the tiny voice added.

At last she settled on a white cotton blouse with fitted short sleeves and open cut-work embroidery in the front and around the stand-up collar. She slipped into a plain black skirt and black hose and pumps and, picking up a short-sleeved linen jacket in her favorite coffee color, stepped back to glance at her reflection. She adjusted the blouse in the waistband of the skirt and reached for her black bag. This would have to do, because there wasn't time for anything else.

Davis pulled his cream-colored Mercedes into the lot behind Southwest's low, rambling administration building and parked near the entrance. He got out and stood leaning against the roof of his car for a moment while he glanced quickly over the other vehicles parked underneath the branches of the small cottonwood trees that had been planted around the carefully landscaped lawn. He had no idea what Tracey's personal car was; she'd been in the zoo's pickup yesterday.

Impatient with himself for the thought, he straightened and tossed his keys in his hand once, then dropped them into his pocket. This was business, he reminded himself for the dozenth time in as many hours. Those fervent topaz eyes and that sensuous mouth could shatter the wall that had surrounded him for the past five years. And he couldn't let that happen. He'd worked too hard to build it.

He was the first thing she saw when she came into the room, and when he looked up and met her eyes the reason she had come to the meeting in the first place threatened to leave her. She had a vague impression that there were several other people in the room, but they were all at a distance, as if they were merely a slightly-out-of-focus background for him.

He was at the head of the broad mahogany table, sitting casually in the big swivel chair, one ankle on the other knee. He was the same, yet entirely different. Now, instead of a dusty cowboy, he was an urbane man-about-town, faultlessly dressed in tan slacks and a pale blue shirt with a navy blazer, his tie discreetly striped in all three colors.

As she hesitated in the doorway he rose and, saying something to the pompous-looking man he'd been talking with, came around the table toward her.

"Hello," he said. "I see you did accept my invitation."

She caught the light woodsy fragrance of his after-shave lotion mixed with the warm masculine scent of him.

"Yes. And I brought some statistics to support my position."

A pulsating silence fell between them, as if each of them had thought of something to say and then rejected it.

Finally he asked, "How's our friend Maqu today? Have you seen him? He hasn't been around my place."

She smiled. "Well, I *hope* he hasn't been around your place again. As a matter of fact, I did drop by to visit him on my lunch hour, and he seemed remarkably mild-mannered, not like himself at all."

His answering smile knocked the breath from her lungs. "He didn't appear to be the type to charge a Jeep?"

She forced herself to breathe. "Not at all. I'm going to ask Dr. Reed whether he could possibly have emotional problems; maybe he's schizoid."

They laughed together, and she relaxed in the warmth that was blossoming between them. The closeness made it seem almost as if they had a history to share—a past that encompassed much more than their brief encounter of the day before.

A sudden coincidental quiet fell over the several different conversations going on in the big room, and she felt eyes on her. She turned and saw that almost everyone was looking at them. For a few seconds Davis didn't notice; then he glanced at the other board members and back to her.

"I suppose it's time to begin the meeting," he said reluctantly. His eyes didn't leave hers. "Why don't you come and sit over here?"

He led her to one of the deep chairs at the side of the table and returned to his place at the end. She sat down and opened her attaché case, but then she couldn't remember what she'd wanted to take out of it.

Finally she put her copy of the proposed budget and a note pad on the table in front of her, conscious of nothing but the smooth, rich tones of Davis's voice as he called the meeting to order.

She doodled with her pen on the pad in front of her and refused to let herself look at him again. This was a business meeting, she lectured herself. She was going to try to get money allocated to the preserve. If she were going to do that, she'd have to stop this insanity.

Davis introduced her to the rest of the board first, and they took care of a few preliminary details. Then they moved on to the major item on the agenda: the budget.

"As you know," Davis said, "the purpose of our meeting tonight is to approve the budget for next year. All of us have already given it a great deal of thought, I'm sure, and we should be able to vote tonight so that none of our proposed new projects will be delayed."

They discussed the total amount and the subtotals for each department; then Davis began to explain the projected sources of income.

"We're hoping to net at least ten percent of this money from visitors' fees," he said, "and the rest will consist of appropriations from the legislatures of our four sponsoring states. You realize, of course, that there's no way to know exactly how much we'll get from them, because the final allocations from New Mexico,

Texas and Oklahoma haven't yet earned final approval. The only amount that's firm so far is Arizona's."

The words soaked in at last, and a thrill of excitement touched her. She hadn't known that there might be extra money to work with! Maybe *it* could be used for the preserve.

She raised her hand to get his attention for her question. "Then it's possible that we'll be receiving more money next year than we have budgeted here?"

He nodded. "It's possible. There probably won't be a great deal more, but there could be some."

"Then I'd like to suggest that we vote to set aside any extra monies that might come in to make additional acquisitions for the preserve." She was relieved that her tone was efficient and professional; she sounded entirely sure that they would agree. Everyone was listening to her carefully.

Encouraged, she went on, "For example, we'd like to start a breeding program for white rhinos, and now that we've purchased one, others need to follow very soon."

Davis chuckled, his blue eyes twinkling at her. "I'm sorry, Tracey. I didn't make myself clear. I didn't mean to imply that we might be getting some sort of a million-dollar windfall. There's no way we'll get enough extra money to begin building up a herd of white rhinos."

His chuckle and the sureness in the phrase "no way" hit her as hard as if he'd slapped her in the face. She stared at him, wide-eyed.

How could he do this to her? How could she have felt just a minute ago that they were close, that they were

sharing something? Now he was dismissing her deepest
concerns with a laugh. And he was patronizing her. He
was treating her as if she were a silly dreamer, as if she
had no sense of business at all.

Hurt and angry bafflement swept through her, and
she stiffened, fighting to keep her voice under control.
"I'm sorry, I must have misunderstood you," she said
evenly. "But if it's true that there will be no substantial
extra income over the next year, then before you vote
to approve this budget the way it stands, you should
search it carefully for funds that could be diverted to
the preserve."

She continued to stare at him for a minute to
emphasize her words, then her gaze swept around the
table, resting briefly on each board member's face.
"We can't wait three years to develop the preserve,"
she went on, her voice lowering with determination as
she warmed to her subject. "The need for captive
breeding of endangered species is urgent; it's the most
important job that zoos have ever been faced with, and
we need to establish Southwest firmly as part of that
movement."

The pudgy man at Davis's left, who had been introduced as Mr. Mattson, bristled. "A great many people
have worked very hard to prepare this budget, Ms.
Johnston," he boomed. "It's too late to start making
changes in it. *And* I assure you that it contains no extra
funds that can be 'diverted,' as you put it."

Tracey's glance flashed back to him. "It contains
some funds for new acquisitions for the display zoo,"

she answered pointedly. "Funds to buy one of a kind. Instead of doing that we should concentrate on fewer species and buy several animals of each of them. Obviously, Mr. Mattson, *that* money is available."

She formed the words carefully, channeling all her feelings into her love for the animals and her work. It was the best way to shut out every thought of Davis Turnbo.

There was a general buzz of conversation around the long table as board members began to express their opinions, and the woman beside Tracey, Mrs. Sheldon, nodded her agreement and leaned over to talk to her.

"You are absolutely right, my dear," she said, patting Tracey's hand. "I've been trying to tell them that since Southwest opened."

Davis called for order. "Let me speak to Tracey's remarks for just a moment," he said. "I don't think any of us needs to be reminded that the legislatures of Arizona, New Mexico, Texas and Oklahoma have helped us establish Southwest with the understanding that we'll be at least fifty percent self-supporting within three years."

He gestured toward his copy of the budget. "The only possible way we can do that is to emphasize the display zoo, encourage tourism and do a lot of public relations work."

"Exactly," Mr. Mattson muttered emphatically, and the woman seated next to Tracey glared at him.

Davis ignored them and went on smoothly. "I have nothing at all against the breeding preserve," he said, looking directly at Tracey. "However, its needs are going to have to be postponed until we can get this institution on its feet financially."

"But three years is a very long time," she answered firmly. She was pleased that her tone was still confident. "There are many species that are on the verge of disappearing now, and in their cases three years could mean the difference between survival and extinction."

"We can't single-handedly save every endangered species in the world, Tracey," he said. "There are several fine institutions in this country, institutions like the San Diego Wild Animal Park and the Arizona-Sonora Desert Museum, that are making big contributions in that area. I want us to join them just as badly as you do, but we're just going to have to wait and do our part when we can afford it."

"But, Davis . . ."

"Tracey, I'm sorry. This is becoming a fruitless argument, and we have several other items on the agenda. I really think we need to end the discussion and vote on the budget."

His tone left no room for disagreement, and before she could reply Mr. Mattson quickly made a motion to take the vote. The majority of the board members voted with him. The budget was approved.

Angrily Tracey leaned back in her chair. She stared at her yellow note pad and fought the disappointment roiling inside her. He hadn't given her a chance! She'd barely presented her case when he had cut her off, and now it was too late. He had very neatly destroyed any hope of changing the budget.

She sat tensely, making a few notes in the margin of her printed agenda about some of the items they discussed and jotting down some observations that she wanted to talk over with Gerald. Everything she did was twice as hard as it normally would have been, and clear thinking was a terrific effort. She filled the margins of the page with doodles, digging her pen fiercely into the defenseless paper.

By the end of the meeting the resentment she'd felt when Davis first countered her suggestion had multiplied a thousand times. And a relentless determination had begun forming in its wake.

No matter what he did, she wasn't going to give up on the money, she thought, drawing big circles at the top of her page of notes. She would come to every board meeting they ever had, if she had to, and ask for funds until they were all sick of hearing about it. The preserve *had* to get under way. Making a contribution to wildlife preservation had been her main purpose in coming to Southwest; this job was her big chance to accomplish something she'd wanted ever since she could remember.

After what seemed like hours the meeting ended, and Tracey began to gather her notes and the useless statistics to put into her attaché case. She wanted nothing now except to get away. She certainly couldn't stand around for a *tête à tête* with Davis as she had before the meeting; she never wanted to be that close to him again. She never wanted to be in the same room with him again.

However, before she could stand, Mrs. Sheldon put a

ringed hand on her arm and held her prisoner in her chair.

"You were so right, my dear," the older woman said. "The money *shouldn't* all go to the display zoo. I don't know when these men will ever wake up and see that we don't have forever to save the poor animals that are threatened by extinction. Why, just the other day I was reading an article about the Argentine pampas deer. . . ." The woman then launched into an incredibly detailed summary of the magazine piece, and there was no way that Tracey could gracefully extricate herself.

She sat, helpless, pretending to listen, wanting to escape, wishing Davis would go ahead and leave. Because in spite of Mrs. Sheldon's spate of words, in spite of every furious remark Tracey had made to herself during the past hour *and* in spite of the fact that she was trying her best to ignore him, she was still more aware of him than of anyone else in the entire room.

She hadn't looked directly at him since he had called for the vote, but the sensual attraction that had pulled her heart into her throat the moment she walked into the room was mixing with her anger to make every inch of her skin an antenna that told her of his whereabouts. While Mrs. Sheldon went on and on Tracey knew, without actually looking in his direction, that Davis, too, had been caught at his place, besieged by the blustering Mr. Mattson. Everyone else was leaving, and soon there would be only the four of them in the room.

Mrs. Sheldon talked steadily on, rattling the wide

silver bangles on her arms as she gestured. Finally, as she stopped for breath Tracey stood and slipped into her jacket. "I really do have to be going," she said. "Maybe you could make a copy of the article for me."

"Come on, Janie," Mr. Mattson boomed from the end of the table, as if Tracey had given a signal. "Let's go get some coffee and let these young folks go home."

"I'd love to," Mrs. Sheldon replied without missing a beat. She turned her most brilliant smile on him and in the space of a second apparently gave up all thoughts of the pampas deer *and* her earlier disapproval of his views. She trilled, "Let's go to Barney's so we can get some croissants, too."

Mr. Mattson came around to take Jane Sheldon's arm, and the two of them told Tracey and Davis good-night as they began walking toward the door. Tracey hurriedly picked up her attaché case and prepared to follow them.

She had taken only a couple of steps, though, when she realized that she didn't have her purse, and without glancing in Davis's direction she went back to her place. Rapidly she sat down again and bent to pick it up from the floor.

When she looked up and swiveled the chair to stand, Davis was close beside her. The soft fabric of his slacks brushed against her leg like a caress.

"I think we should go for coffee, too," he said, "don't you?"

Chapter Three

Her chest tightened painfully. This time his eyes were exactly the color of the pale blue of his shirt, and the faint scent of his cologne was drifting to her again.

Then anger flared in her stomach, and for a few seconds she couldn't answer. How could he dare suggest such a thing when he'd just ruined her efforts to get funding? He had effectively stopped everything she'd tried to do; he'd contradicted everything she'd said. Did he think that now they could overlook it all and be friends?

Well, he could forget it. She'd never go anywhere with him!

"We don't have to go to Barney's," he went on, his lips curving warmly. "That probably isn't your first choice of restaurants at this very minute."

In spite of her frustration the remark tugged the

corners of her mouth into a tiny smile. "No, I don't think so," she agreed. "I'm afraid I'd have to hear every word of the rest of Janie's article."

She stood, and when her shoulder grazed his chest she moved quickly around him.

"We could drive out to the Mariposa," he said. "I doubt that anyone there has ever even heard of the Argentine pampas deer." His smile was almost magically persuasive.

She looked away to keep from falling under its spell. "No, thank you, I really have to go."

She walked toward the door, intending to leave him behind, but he turned and fell into step with her, strolling beside her as if she had said yes instead of no to his invitation. He was so sure of himself that it was infuriating.

"Tracey, we need to talk," he said as he held the heavy door open for her.

She went through it quickly. "I don't know why," she snapped. "We've both talked quite a bit this evening, and neither of us has said one thing the other can agree to."

"Neither one of us wanted to go to Barney's," he retorted, triumph in his tone.

Against her will she chuckled, stopping short to look up at him. He was grinning at her impishly, as if she had no reason at all to be angry with him.

She sighed, completely exasperated. "Davis, you know what I mean. It's pointless for us to spend time together, because we're at totally opposite ends of the spectrum on this whole subject of priorities for Southwest. This is extremely important to me, and you deliberately destroyed any progress I might have made tonight."

Abruptly she walked on to her little dark blue Datsun and opened the door so she could throw her case inside. But before she could get in, too, he was beside her. "You're looking at this all wrong," he said earnestly. "I want the preserve—"

"My work is the most important thing in my life, Davis," she interrupted coldly, "and you're making it really difficult for me."

"But I don't mean to," he answered. "And that's why you should go with me to the Mariposa and talk. I need to explain my point of view so you'll have a better opinion of me." He smiled into her eyes. "I know from the way you looked at me during the meeting tonight that you think I'm in the same class with the people who kill baby seals."

She didn't reply.

He placed one hand on the roof of her car, his arm only inches from hers. The desert evening was cool and quiet; the faint noises of the animals in the zoo enclosures floated to them on the still air.

The only coherent thought in her mind was that she had to get away from him. He was making her crazy. She was furious with him; he had betrayed the instant of closeness they'd had a couple of hours ago, and now she was trying to tear her eyes away from his broad chest, wondering what it would be like to run her hands over its muscular bulk.

"Tracey, let me convince you that you're wrong

about me," he said, his voice very low. "I'm really on the same side you are; it's just that you don't see that yet."

She looked up, startled. "Well, you could've fooled me and anybody else who was at that meeting just now," she shot back. "If we're on the same side now, I'd certainly hate for us to be enemies."

She turned to reach for the handle of the car door. His broad, hard hand caught her wrist and turned her to face him.

"So would I," he said. His voice was resonant with feeling and with a significance that seemed to give the simple words a double meaning. It was as warm as the shock of his fingertips against the inside of her wrist, and, suddenly weak, she didn't pull away.

She let him close the door of her car and seat her in the solid comfort of the Mercedes, but as he slid into the driver's seat her resentment flared again. She welcomed it as if it were an old friend. She had to cling to *something,* and anger certainly made more sense than this irrational attraction that was making her eyes linger on his lean hands as they gripped the wheel, this inexplicable magnetism that was making her so painfully aware of his warm nearness.

With an effort she turned away and stared out into the night. "This is a waste of time," she said testily. "I have an early day tomorrow, and I need to go over some papers before then."

He chuckled, a low, rich sound deep in his throat that drew her eyes back to him. "Don't worry," he said, his eyes holding hers as he started the motor and put the car into gear. A wry smile curved his lips under the heavy mustache. "You aren't wasting a minute. We're going to begin getting acquainted so we can work together."

"I see no hope of that," she retorted. "At the board meeting just now we couldn't have been further apart."

He turned away and backed the car out of its space. "Nevertheless we have to learn to get along," he said, concern replacing the teasing tone that had just been in his voice. "If Gerald doesn't come back for a month or more, you and I are going to be running Southwest."

"Oh, but he'll surely be back before too long!" Somehow she hadn't let herself think that Gerald might really be so ill that she'd have to take over his responsibilities for any length of time.

"I talked with him today," he replied as he pulled onto the highway. "It's possible that he'll have to rest for six to eight weeks."

Her eyes widened. She wasn't ready for this. She needed to learn how to be *assistant* administrator before she could function as administrator.

"Well, maybe he'll recover much sooner than he thinks," she said hopefully.

He shrugged. "Maybe."

She tried to put her mind on something else. Tonight of all times she didn't need any more problems. "Why did you say the two of us might be running Southwest?" she asked. "What about the rest of the board?"

His eyes flashed back to hers, and the engaging grin touched his lips again. "They pretty well do as I say."

His tone was flat with an unshakable confidence, and

the image of him astride the palomino flashed through her mind. She'd been right in her first estimation of him, she thought. He did consider himself boss of the world. Well, he'd see. She was one person who wouldn't do as he said. He might be chairman of the board, but she wasn't going to sacrifice a single one of her ideals.

They talked only in generalities as they completed the short drive to the Mariposa, and as they parked and went in she began to marshal her arguments again. If she was going to be there, she might as well try again to make some progress in changing his mind.

However, once they were seated in the pleasant atmosphere of the luxurious club-restaurant, the unsettling awareness of being near him grew stronger again, and she had trouble remembering what she wanted to say. In the dim light his eyes looked very blue against his tanned skin, and from time to time his knee brushed against hers in the small, curved booth.

The waitress appeared, and Davis asked, "Coffee?"

Tracey nodded.

"And how about some nachos? Are you hungry?"

She looked up into his eyes again, and suddenly a sensation of emptiness, almost a dizziness, swept through her. She was starving. But for a minute she couldn't think about food. Then she said, "Why, yes. I suppose so. I didn't have time to eat before the meeting."

"Neither did I." He ordered, and then turned to her, placing his arm along the back of the booth, his fingers almost touching her shoulder as he relaxed.

"So your work is the most important thing in your life," he said speculatively, holding her gaze with his own. "Very interesting."

She stiffened as she recalled her earlier impassioned statement and the emotions that had prompted it. "I don't think that's so unusual," she said. "I'm sure that's true of a lot of people."

He quirked one sandy eyebrow and looked away as the waitress poured their coffee. "Probably. It's just that somehow I didn't expect to hear that from . . ."

"From whom?" she challenged.

He shrugged helplessly. "From such an absolutely beautiful woman."

Her hands trembled at his words and at the sincerity that deepened his voice as he said them, but she protested. "Davis, that remark is . . ."

He held up one hand. "Chauvinistic. I knew you'd say that, but I had to be honest. I couldn't think of a lie fast enough." He smiled his apology, and she would have forgiven him anything.

"And what's wrong with work being the most important thing in a person's life, man or woman?"

He sipped some of the coffee and then turned the cup in his big fingers. "Oh . . . nothing. I didn't mean to imply that there was something wrong with it. As a matter of fact, it's true of me, too."

"Your work and Southwest," she said, appraising him in turn. "Not your family?"

His eyes blazed at her, filled with a terrible pain; then his face closed and hardened. She wished desperately that she hadn't asked the question. But she couldn't have known. Why would the mention of a family bring that look to his eyes? What had happened? What or who had hurt him so?

He took another drink. "I don't have a family," he said quickly, almost harshly. "How do you like Arizona?"

"Fine," she managed, thrown off balance by his reaction to her question and the quick change of subject. She looked at him questioningly for a second and then down into the brown liquid in her cup.

"This is your first job, isn't it?"

His tone had lost its harshness; now it was flat, totally businesslike. In spite of the quiet ambience of the room and the mood music that the pianist was playing, it made her feel as if she were in an office interviewing for her job all over again.

"Yes."

"I thought I remembered reading that in your résumé, and some of the things you said in the meeting tonight reminded me." He paused thoughtfully, his blue eyes boring into hers. "Tracey, it takes a while to get adjusted to the real world once you leave the idealistic atmosphere of school. I think you ought to give yourself more time to get things into perspective before you ask for too many big changes at Southwest."

She stared at him, wide-eyed. "Big changes like money for the breeding program?"

"Well, yes." His voice was smoother now, more persuasive, and he offered her some of the nachos that the waitress had just brought. "After you've been here a little longer you'll realize that—"

"Davis, come to the point. What are you really trying to tell me?" She tried to hold her voice steady.

"That your goals and your ideas are great, but you aren't seeing reality where they're concerned. You've got to learn to read facts and figures, dollars and cents, and believe what they tell you."

The waitress came back with baskets of crisp chips and guacamole dip, picante sauce and hot tortillas, but suddenly Tracey wasn't hungry anymore. The chairman of the board that controlled her job was telling her that she was being completely unreasonable.

"I can read," she answered, fury rising in her by the minute. "And I *can* see reality. Reality is the fact that whole species are being wiped out all over the world while we sit around and . . . eat nachos!"

He grinned as he bit into one.

"Don't patronize me, Davis! I've loved animals and studied them all my life, and I'm perfectly qualified to do my job!"

He nodded. "But right now you're doing Gerald's job, and someday you may want it or one like it on a permanent basis. You'll never be able to do that unless you give up this fairy-tale attitude of yours that everything you want can somehow miraculously be accomplished overnight."

She was astounded. "I do *not* have a fairy-tale attitude! And I'm not expecting miracles; I know that building a breeding preserve takes time. But that's the very reason we need to get started!" Anger pounded in her temples; then desperation flooded in its wake.

If this was his attitude, if he wouldn't take her

seriously, if the board members really did usually do what he told them, then they could make her job a nightmare. They could make her wait years and years to reach the goals she'd already waited a lifetime for.

Her topaz eyes, brimming with anger and hurt, held his for a long minute; then he looked away, silently cursing his efforts. He'd only wanted to help her learn to cope with the financial facts, to try to erase that surprised frustration he'd seen on her face during the meeting, but he hadn't accomplished that. Instead he'd made everything worse.

Well, he might have known he'd botch it. He'd never known how to make a woman happy. Marla had proved that beyond a doubt.

Flinching away from the painful memories that had been haunting him lately, he met Tracey's fiery eyes. "Look, let's talk about it another time, all right? We've both had a long hard day, and we're in no shape for an argument. I chose the wrong time to bring this up."

She shook her head and tried to find the words to defend herself, but her head was pounding with emotion and her thoughts were a jumble.

"I mean it, Tracey," he was saying firmly. "I didn't intend to upset you. Let's just forget it and have something to eat."

"I can't forget it," she said. "And I don't want anything to eat. Please take me back to my car now."

They drove back through the cool night in an uncomfortable near-silence. He parked near her car and came around to open her door and help her out.

"Tracey, I'm sorry if I was undiplomatic," he said

quietly. "I just want to keep you from being hurt and disappointed as you begin to see what we're up against."

"Well, as I see the obstacles I'm going to overcome them," she told him, her eyes blazing up into his. "You'll see that I'm realistic enough to get this preserve under way in spite of everything!" He didn't answer. "Davis . . ."

But the expression in his eyes had changed, and she knew that he was no longer thinking about their disagreement or about Southwest. He was thinking about nothing but her.

She couldn't go on, she'd lost the thread of what she had intended to say. She couldn't take her eyes away from his face in the pale moonlight, from the potent magnetism of his burning gaze. He was looking at her as if he were memorizing something about her, as if he were as powerless as she was to look away.

The faint moonlight sprinkled her face with a silver sheen, and his eyes followed its movements, absorbing every feature that it touched: her arched brows, her slightly tilted nose, her strong cheekbones. Then it played along her lips and pulled their bodies closer together, although neither of them was conscious of the movement.

He reached out to her; he cupped her chin in his fingers to run his thumb over her mouth's full ripeness. He took his hand away and slowly, slowly bent his head to hers. His lips brushed across hers lightly once, then again.

Sharp hunger stabbed through him. He pulled back,

fighting it, trying to remember what he had resolved, the rules he had lived by for the last few years. Her lips were warm and trembling, though, and her eyes were incredibly alive under her thick curling lashes.

He bent to take her lips, and with a shattered sigh she moved even closer, her body hesitantly touching, then melting against his.

He intensified the kiss, and his hands eagerly began to explore, caressing her back, her shoulders, the curve of her rounded hips, pressing her to him with all the longing that had been pulling at him since the minute he had seen her with her hair blowing in the wind.

The touch, then the incredible intimacy of his long body against hers, filled her senses. Instinctively she moved even closer. She ran her fingers through his hair in a silent plea for his lips to press more firmly against hers; then, as the electric heat of his tongue touched her mouth, she ran her hands down his neck and over the expanse of his shoulders.

The ripple of his muscles under the thin fabrics of his jacket and shirt made her tremble; the palms of her hands ached with the desire to stroke his bare skin.

His mouth moved over hers, kissing each corner, each part of it separately, carefully, as if he wanted to experience and remember every individual sensation. Then he took it with his own as if he were laying claim to it forever.

His tongue slid along her lower lip, then the upper one; then it glided into her mouth, demanding entrance. It dipped into her mouth again and again, while one of his hands tangled itself into the masses of her hair. The other found the curve of her waist under the loose jacket.

Her tongue met his and welcomed it, and they touched and withdrew over and over, taking and giving, building the fire. The rhythm of their caresses increased steadily until a glowing desire shimmered through her and a cry began to repeat itself in her brain.

She wanted him; she wanted him. The words pounded in her blood, in the beat of her pulse, in the shaking of her fingers as they returned to stroke his neck and the side of his cheek. Then she pulled away just slightly to slip her hands under his jacket and run them over the breadth of his chest, resenting again the barrier of clothing that was between them.

When she moved his mouth followed hers as if he were afraid of losing her, and he increased the tempo of the kiss. The depth of it, the movement, became so erotic that a white bolt of desire burst in her.

It was so potent that it terrified her. She wanted him more than she had ever wanted anything; she wanted his body, and she wanted his closeness. She wanted this passion for all her life.

But this was only for a moment, a second.

She stiffened and wrenched her mouth from his, dropping her arms to push his away. Her frantic movements were a surprise, and before he could pro-test, she was gone. She turned and leapt into the little car all in the same moment and drove very fast out of the lot.

He stood in the pool of shadow cast by the cotton-wood trees and watched her go, a sudden sharp feeling of loneliness and frustration filling him. What the hell did he think he was doing? he asked himself bitterly. Why had he even taken her out? Why was he worrying about her feelings, anyway? That was exactly what he'd sworn never to do again.

After she'd turned onto the highway that led to Tucson and the sound of her car had died away, he walked to the Mercedes and jerked its door open in a gesture that was as savage as his scowl.

When she drove into the driveway of her house she turned off the motor and just sat, leaning her forehead against the hardness of the steering wheel. She hardly knew how she'd gotten home. She couldn't remember any of the fifteen miles of highway that she'd driven.

All she remembered was Davis's lips on hers and the unaccustomed intimacy of his chest against her breasts. She ran her tongue along her lips, and she could almost taste the tip of his tongue against hers.

She let all the sensations flow through her, and with them came the rush of desire that she'd felt when she was in his arms. The feeling filled her again, and for a moment she savored it. She'd forgotten how complete-ly wonderful it was to be held, to be so close to someone.

Or maybe she'd never known. Even with Eric, somehow it had never been like that.

Restlessly she straightened, the fear clutching at her

once more. Eric. He'd given her her first real taste of affection, what she'd thought at the time was love, and dating him had made her feel as if she had someone of her own at last. Someone to love her after all the childhood years of trying to get attention and love from indifferent relatives who were too busy even to notice what she needed.

But Eric had been no better. That security and happiness had lasted less than a year, less than her last nine months at college. And for a year after they broke up she'd suffered terribly.

His handsome young face came back to her clearly; she let herself see it for the first time in months. Now that she was past so much of the hurt she wished that she could remember him as he had been when they were happy. But the only picture her mind seemed to hold of him was of the last time she had seen him, the night he'd broken their engagement. His soft gray eyes had been filled with guilt and pain as he'd told her that he couldn't resist his parents' insistence that he marry his childhood sweetheart.

Now he seemed so unbelievably boyish when she compared him with Davis Turnbo. Davis's face held a strength, a confidence and a determination that Eric's would never have. She pictured Davis in the moonlight, looking deep into her eyes, trying to see into her thoughts, an expression in his eyes and on his rugged face that she couldn't quite name. It had been a look almost of vulnerability, of some sort of wariness that came from deep within.

And his face in the meeting . . . He'd been so mas-

terful, so much in control, so completely sure of himself
and his opinions.

She sat up very straight, gathered her things and got
out of the car. *That's* what she'd better remember
about Davis Turnbo. He was in control of Southwest,
and he was doing everything he could to stymie her
work. She would never reach her goals with him
destroying everything she tried to do.

She walked rapidly across the peaceful yard, throw-
ing her jacket around her shoulders against the desert's
night chill. The sounds of the horses moving around
floated to her, and she smiled when Foxfire, her
Morgan mare, nickered "hello." Animals had been her
only friends for so many years, and that horse and
Geoffrey, the Old English sheepdog she'd had since her
college Chaucer course, had been her real family for
the past few years.

She walked across the long back patio and stepped
over Geoffrey, who lay in his favorite place across the
door, to flip the light on inside the kitchen. The Spanish
tiles on the counter reflected the glow from the cast-
iron wall sconces, and the plants in the sill of the open
window moved a little in the breeze. Everything was
just as it had been when she left it, but nothing seemed
the same. She stood for a minute in the middle of the
big room, trying to wipe out all thoughts of Davis and
his kiss, trying to get back into her old life.

She moved into the living room and put her purse
and attaché case on the heavy low chest by the couch.
She went into the bedroom, stripped off her clothes and
took the pale yellow nightgown from just inside the

closet. It had been a terrifically long day, and if she could just go to sleep, everything would be back to normal tomorrow.

She brushed her teeth and hair, then wound the thick strands into a knot on top of her head and ran the tub full of hot water, pouring her favorite scented crystals into the stream. A bubble bath would relax her, and when she went to bed Davis Turnbo would be the farthest thing from her mind.

But instead he was the closest thing to it as she slid into the spicy-smelling water and took the loofah from its place above the soap dish. She could visualize his blue eyes looking at her with that same fire she'd seen in them when he bent to kiss her; she could feel the tantalizing touch of his tongue on hers.

Frowning, she soaped her back thoroughly, then her arms and her long legs, trying not to imagine what it would be like for his big hands to do that for her. She couldn't think about him, couldn't wish for his kiss again; she had to forget his touch.

What was wrong with her, anyway? she asked herself impatiently. Had those few minutes of shattering desire for him stripped away all the defenses she'd built around the fierce feelings and the need to be loved that had always been a part of her?

She couldn't let that happen. No matter how strong her emotions were, she had to channel them in other directions, to keep them repressed as she'd been doing since Eric's desertion. Her emotions always ran too strong for casual relationships, and so-called permanent ones never lasted, so it was better simply not to get involved.

She'd been alone all her childhood, and she knew how to cope with that; it was best for her. It left her free to pour everything into her work and her ambitions to reach her goals. She'd wanted this job since she'd been big enough to know that such things as animal preserves existed, and getting involved with Davis could ruin everything she'd worked so hard for.

After her bath she slipped into the nightgown and loosened her hair until it fell around her face, but she didn't go immediately to bed. Instead she stood for a long time at the casement window of her room, looking out across the little place that in these past few months had become her home.

The pale moon was higher now; its rays were touching the mesquite trees at the edge of the yard and outlining the low roof of the stables, and the night was quieter than she could ever have believed. Everything was still but her heart, and it was shouting a message at her that she didn't want to hear.

Chapter Four

Tracey took a deep breath as she returned the receiver to its cradle on her desk. She stared at it for a minute.

Well, *that* news ought to be enough to get her mind off Davis Turnbo, she thought. All morning she'd been fighting the memory of his arms around her the night before, trying desperately not to think about him even though her lips still burned with the memory of his. Those overpowering remembered sensations had kept coming between her and the papers on her desk in spite of all her efforts to concentrate.

Now she'd *have* to banish them. She was going to be acting as administrator of Southwest for at least three weeks longer, and probably more. Doing that well was going to take every ounce of concentration and energy that she had.

Uneasily she ran one hand through her hair, and with the other she punched the button that signaled Lottie. "Did you talk to Gerald, too?" she asked as soon as the secretary came in. "Did he tell you the news?"

"If you mean the news that our fearless leader won't be returning until goodness knows when, yes, I heard."

"Oh, Lottie, how could this happen right now? I need him here to help me raise support for the breeding program!" She began ruffling through the stack of papers in front of her. "I need him to decide what to do about this incredible donation for some snow leopards; I need him to attend this meeting of the Animal Protection Association instead of my having to go. I need him to talk to the representatives of the Zoo-keepers Organization!" She took a deep breath and gave Lottie a beseeching look. "I need him here to do his job so I can be free to do mine!"

Lottie responded to the tirade with a wry chuckle. "I can't think of a single reason why *I* need him to come back," she said. "But I do see your problem."

Tracey smiled in spite of her frustration. "All right, if you're going to be so calm about this, I'm going to give you some extra duties. You can just meet with the zookeepers yourself."

Lottie waved the idea away. "Not that crew," she said. "I'd do it only if they all looked like the guy who's waiting to see you right now."

"I didn't know someone was waiting. Who is it?"

"Cody Howard. You know, the boy from that young felons program."

"Oh, yes. I saw those papers just a minute ago,"

Tracey said as she went back through the stack. She found them. "He's to work here for six months in order to get the charges against him dropped," she read. "He was involved in some kind of a brawl."

"With Richard Barnes—which is, no doubt, the only reason he was ever arrested in the first place," Lottie said cynically. In response to Tracey's questioning look she explained. "Daddy Barnes owns the half of Arizona that doesn't belong to Davis Turnbo. He has all kinds of influence in this state."

Tracey tried to ignore the acceleration of her pulse-beat at the sound of Davis's name. "So I'm to decide which job to give him for six months," she mused aloud. "I need to think about that. You might be wrong, Lottie; he might really be a troublemaker."

"Not him," Lottie insisted. "Anybody that beautiful can't be anything but good."

Tracey chuckled. "I'm not sure that looks are the best criterion for judging behavior, Lottie. Maybe I should put him in the kitchen, where Sonny Lawrence would be his supervisor. Sonny's big enough to handle anything."

"You could. But you could also assign him to help me. I really need an assistant."

Tracey laughed. "Lottie, I'm beginning to think you're a dirty old woman. Go out there and tell this wonder boy of yours to come in."

Cody was every bit as handsome as Lottie had said, with a copper complexion and high cheekbones that spoke of American Indian blood. His dark eyes held a mixture of streetwise charm and loneliness that caught

at Tracey, and the smile he gave her as Lottie introduced them was whimsically contagious.

"That Maqu is really something, isn't he?" was the
way he greeted Tracey, and that, combined with his
smile, immediately won her heart.

"He is. Have you just come from seeing him?"

"Yes. I got here early. I've always liked to hang
around the zoo. When I was a kid I used to go to the old
one all the time and pretend that I was taking care of
the animals."

The unconscious loneliness in the remark and in his
voice reminded Tracey of herself as a child. "And you
still read the signs on each exhibit."

"Right. How can I come visit these guys if I don't
know their names?"

She laughed. "I agree. Zoos are much more fun
when everyone's on a first-name basis."

Since he'd mentioned Maqu, she told him the story
of the escape and recapture, and he asked, "Won't he
be moved into the preserve soon? Don't you have an
enclosure there that's a whole lot like his real home?"

She looked at him appraisingly. He'd obviously been
keeping up with the plans for Southwest as they were
discussed in the media, and he was genuinely interested.

"We do. But I don't know exactly when we'll get to
move him. He's in the display zoo right now so he'll
draw more visitors; there's been quite a bit of publicity
about our getting him."

"I know. I've been hearing a lot about it."

She fiddled with the papers on her desk while her

mind whirled, making a fast decision. Cody was clearly interested in animals and in the zoo and preserve, and that enthusiasm could prove to be contagious. He was neatly groomed, and his good looks and natural charm would draw people to him and to the things he told them. And the group of new volunteer guides for the zoo's tours was pitifully small.

She took a deep breath. "Cody, for the six months you'll be with us I'd like you to be a guide at the display zoo. You'll take training classes for a few days, and then you'll lead groups of visitors through the zoo. For now it's just the zoo, because the preserve isn't really under way yet."

His eyes glowed, and his smile warmed her. "I'd like that," he told her. "I'll do a good job for you."

She smiled back. "I know you will, Cody. Report to Madeleine Custer, our education curator, tomorrow morning at 9:30. She'll show you the ropes."

"I'll be there. Thanks, Ms. Johnston."

When he had gone Tracey sat back in her chair and stared out her window down the winding drive that led to the African Savanna Exhibit. She picked up a pen and absently whirled it around in her fingers, wondering whether she'd done the right thing.

Of course she had, she told herself. Cody was a lonely kid who turned to animals for affection just as she had always done. He'd even had the same dreams she'd had of working with them someday.

But a tiny doubt nagged at her. Cody *couldn't* let her down by getting into a fight with a visitor, or some other trouble! If he did, not only would she never hear the last of it from Gerald, but also Davis Turnbo would be yelling that she lived in a fantasy world for sure.

She left her desk and walked out to Lottie's. "Well, you were right. Cody is beautiful," she teased as she picked up a thin sheaf of messages that had come in. "But I'm afraid he's too young for you."

"I know," Lottie said with an exaggerated sigh, not looking up from her typing. "More's the pity."

Tracey looked through her messages and stopped when she found one from the nursery director. She would have loved to get out of the office for a few minutes and let her head clear while she sorted out her priorities and prepared for Gerald's absence.

"Lottie, I'm going over to the main nursery to check on the new infant chimp," she said. "And on the way back I'll stop by the snack area and see if it's all geared up for the busy season."

"Okay. If it's about lunch time when you come back, would you bring me a tuna salad sandwich? I'm going to spend my lunch hour typing your speech."

Tracey snapped her fingers. "I'd forgotten about that speech! When is it?"

The secretary glanced at her calendar. "Chamber of Commerce, Phoenix, noon, next Monday."

"All right. Be sure not to schedule too much that day so I'll have time to drive over and back."

Lottie nodded, and Tracey turned and started out of the room. "I'll bring your sandwich. Such devotion to duty deserves a reward. I'll even bring you a soda, too."

But once she was outside, instead of thinking about the specifics of her work she just enjoyed the idea of it. She was surrounded by nearly two thousand acres to be used to save threatened animal species, and to entertain and educate people who were interested in those animals, and the thought made her shiver a little in spite of the heat. She was established at last in the career she'd always dreamed of.

She strolled along, absorbing the brilliant colors of the mariposa lilies and golden poppies that had been planted in masses along the gravel paths and driveways, and taking in the details of every exhibit that she passed. When she arrived at the nursery she threw herself into holding and playing with the chimp and two little spider monkeys wearing diapers with holes cut for their tails to go through.

The nursery director even let her feed them, and by the time she'd finished and put them back into their playpen with the blankets that were their surrogate mothers, it was almost noon.

She made her way toward the snack bar through the groups of tourists strolling the grounds, noticing happily that there were many more now than she'd seen when she came over.

The outdoor restaurant seemed to be in fine shape for the rush season, and since they were already busy, she didn't take up the manager's time to talk business. Instead she took one of the few empty tables in the shade and ordered an iced tea. She sipped at the cool drink and began to make a mental list of nursery animals that could be transferred to the Children's Zoo.

"Tracey."

The low masculine voice stopped the breath in her throat and froze her fingers around the glass. For a long minute the shadows of the leaves on the cottonwood trees stopped shifting over the tabletop, and the only motion in the world was the beating of her heart.

When she looked up at last even that ceased.

Davis was standing beside her table, relaxed and casual in jeans and a tan knit shirt. It fit him to perfection and, of their own free will, her eyes roved slowly over his broad chest, his shoulders and his face, barely meeting his blue eyes.

Then, still without conscious direction, her gaze moved to the girl beside him.

She was so beautiful that she was breathtaking. Her hair was the palest possible shade of red, sleekly styled to fall around her face; her porcelain skin was as delicate as the color of her hair.

"Tracey, this is Peggy Smalley. I was just bringing her over to your office to meet you." He turned to the girl. "Peggy, this is Tracey Johnston."

"Hello. Won't you sit down?" Tracey felt herself smile and heard her own voice before she knew she was going to speak.

Davis held one of the wrought-iron chairs for Peggy, and she sat directly across from Tracey. She gave Tracey a dazzling, assured smile. Her eyes were a lively gray-green.

Frantically Tracey tried to force her mind to function. She should know who the girl was. The name Peggy Smalley was one that she had come into contact with recently, but now she couldn't remember when or how.

Then it came to her. The internship program for college students! That, like the young felons program, was one of Gerald's projects to establish good community relations and to generate publicity for Southwest. Peggy Smalley was going to work for her.

Tracey took a sip of her drink. "I've been expecting you," she told the girl. "You're from Easton College, aren't you?"

"Yes. I'm doing my senior internship this summer."

Davis had taken the chair between them and was signaling the waitress. Tracey's glance went to him and then back to Peggy. "I had no idea that you two knew each other," she said.

"Oh, we've known each other for years and years, haven't we, Davis?" Peggy fastened her huge black-fringed eyes on him. "Ever since I can remember."

Davis flashed her a quick smile. "I think I can remember a time before *I* knew *you,* but I'm not quite sure," he teased.

While he was ordering cold drinks for the two of them, Peggy leaned confidingly toward Tracey. "Davis has talked about Southwest so much," she said. "And it's so important to him that I do my internship here. I think I would've just died if it hadn't worked out."

Tracey tried to remember the application forms she'd once skimmed hurriedly. "You aren't a zoology major, are you?"

"No, business. At Easton the requirements are just

that we have to have the experience of working for one summer, at anything at all, and I wanted Southwest." She glanced at Davis with a conspirator's smile.

He smiled back and then turned to Tracey. "How's your day going?" he asked casually.

She looked down and took a sip of tea. This was the first time she'd seen him since he'd melted her with his kisses, yet both his look and his words were completely offhand. *He* certainly hadn't lain awake last night thinking about *her*.

"Fine," she answered. "I've just come from the nursery; there are some of the cutest baby spider monkeys over there."

"I always enjoy watching the babies, but I haven't been by the nursery for a while," he said. "I've been so busy lately I'm afraid Southwest has been about last on my list."

"Davis, would you take me over to the nursery later?" Peggy broke in. "I'll bet the babies are so cute! Oh, maybe I could work there!"

Davis turned to Tracey as the waitress brought drinks for him and Peggy. "Peggy can't wait to know what job she'll have for the summer," he said, "and we thought maybe you could tell us today, even though she isn't supposed to report until Monday."

Peggy nodded enthusiastic agreement, her hair swinging softly around her cheeks. "I'd love to work in the nursery," she repeated, "or maybe I can do something related to P. R. work."

"P. R. would probably be better," Tracey answered,

giving Peggy a long, appraising look. "The nursery sounds like lots of fun, but you'd have to have some experience with animals first."

Davis was leaning back in his chair, listening carefully. He was playing with his straw, rolling it over and over on the tabletop with his long tanned fingers. The crisp curling hairs on the back of his hand glinted golden in the sunlight.

Tracey pulled her eyes back to Peggy's face. "It isn't always fun to work in the nursery. You have to diaper and clean up after baby animals, and struggle to teach them to eat, and you have to be really strong emotionally to cope with the ones who are ill and die."

Peggy wrinkled her pretty nose. "Then I agree with you. I think public relations would be better for me."

"I think we could arrange that," Tracey told her. "We really need people on the tour guide staff right now."

Peggy sipped her drink, frowning a little. "I might like that, but I wouldn't know what to say about the animals I'd be showing."

Tracey smiled. "We don't choose our guides on the basis of how much they know about animals," she teased. "We choose the ones with strong legs and tons of patience."

Peggy smiled back and scooted her chair away from the table a little so she could unfold one long leg for their inspection. "I don't know about the tons of patience, but I think my legs will be okay, don't you, Davis?"

He looked her leg over thoroughly from beneath his

sleepy-looking eyelids. "Definitely," he answered. "I'd say they're more than okay."

Peggy's legs were as smoothly beautiful as the rest of her, and her foot was neatly enclosed in an espadrille one shade darker than her lavender walking shorts and matching designer shirt. Her overall appearance was so stylish and perfect that Tracey glanced down at her own rather unremarkable navy blue slacks and white shirt under her short jacket. She'd worn a smock to help with the zoo babies, but now she felt rumpled and disheveled anyway.

She looked up at Davis. He took a sip of his drink, then held the rim of the glass against his lip for a moment, apparently thinking, his eyes on hers. Then he looked back at Peggy.

"Peggy'll have a good time on the guide staff," he teased. "She loves to talk more than anyone I've ever known, and in that job she'll have a captive audience."

His kidding grin made his lips curve appealingly under the sweeping mustache. Heat spread through Tracey as she remembered the taste of them against her own, and all the piercing sensations she had felt in his arms began pulling at her again. With an effort she transferred her eyes from his face to the gleaming top of the table.

Peggy laughed and tapped Davis lightly on the wrist, her fingers very pale against his tanned skin. "Now, Davis, that isn't true," she chided. "You know I don't talk half as much as Marquita does."

He laughed, too, a full rich sound. "Marquita is my housekeeper of many years' standing," he explained to

Tracey. "And there have been times when I've threatened to run away from home because of her chatter." His blue eyes glinted with amusement. "I've had to hire two maids and a gardener just so she'll have somebody else to talk to."

Tracey tried to absorb that information. How did Peggy know Marquita so well? Was she spending the summer at Davis's house? Who was she, anyway, and what was she to him?

Whatever she was, he'd come to Southwest to find out what her job would be for the summer. He hadn't come to see Tracey.

She'd thought of him a thousand times since last night, but those few minutes with her had certainly made no memories for him, she thought. Evidently he'd forgotten all about them.

And the sooner she followed his example, the better, she told herself fiercely as he and Peggy bantered lightly about the duties of a tour guide. He'd told her the evening before that she was living in a fantasy world, and any thoughts of the two of them together fit that description exactly.

She chatted with them for a few minutes more; then, as soon as she could, she signaled the waitress and asked for Lottie's order. When it came she stood up. "I have to go now," she said. "Peggy, I'll be out of town until about 3:00 on Monday, so why don't you just come in that morning and report to Madeleine Custer, our education curator? She'll get your training started."

"I will," Peggy answered. "And thank you, Tracey."

Her smile and her firm handshake made her even more likeable. "It was good to meet you."

"It was good to meet you. I'll see you soon."

Davis was standing, too, his tall form dwarfing Tracey's. He touched her arm lightly in good-bye, and she tried to suppress the disturbing exhilaration it stirred in her.

"I'll see you, Tracey." His tone was somehow intimate, too intimate for Peggy to hear, and Tracey walked away from them with her blood pounding in her ears.

Tracey pulled her little car into the space marked "Johnston" and turned off the motor. She sat for a minute or two, just relaxing after the long drive from Phoenix.

She really ought to go into her office and see what messages had accumulated during the day, she knew, but suddenly that seemed the dullest possible choice for the rest of the afternoon. Her speech had gone well, and had generated a lot of questions and perhaps some new support for Southwest, and that had fired her enthusiasm for her work to an even higher pitch than usual. Now she wanted to visit the animals themselves instead of taking care of the paperwork connected with them. Also, she thought, taking in the brightness of the flowers in the sunlight, the winding paths that fanned out from the administration building were much more inviting than its four walls.

She succumbed to temptation and joined the many visitors who were wandering through the grounds. She had almost passed the African Savanna Exhibit when she realized that the group of people standing in front of it were together in a tour and that Cody was their leader.

She stood in the background and listened, smiling at the handsome, confident picture he made in his khaki-colored uniform. "No, the gazelles can't escape," he was saying. "They don't think 'up'—they think 'straight ahead,' and they'd probably run right into the wall and break their necks before they'd jump over it."

There was a buzz of interested comments, and Tracey was listening to them when she heard someone calling her name. She turned. Peggy was striding toward her, a frown wrinkling her delicate face.

"Tracey, I need to talk with you," the girl said worriedly. "I was just on my way over to your office."

"Hello, Peggy. What's wrong?"

"Oh, I'm so upset," the girl answered in a tone that implied they were old friends. "But I don't know whether I can talk about it here."

"We could go back to the office," Tracey said, "but it's so much more pleasant outdoors." She glanced around and saw a shaded bench. "Why don't we sit over there and talk?"

Peggy looked quickly toward Cody and his group, who were walking away from them; then she nodded. As soon as the two of them were seated she leaned toward Tracey earnestly, her gray-green eyes very wide. "I just can't believe this!" she declared.

"Can't believe what?"

"That I've come all the way across the country to do

my internship and I'm expected to work with people like that!"

Tracey stared at her. "People like what? Whom are you talking about, Peggy?"

"People like him—that guide who just left. You know the one. Madeleine assigned me as his partner, and then she said he was working here instead of going to jail. He's a criminal!"

"Oh, Cody!" Tracey exclaimed. "Are you talking about Cody Howard?"

"Yes." Peggy's tone was sure and full of disapproval. "That's his name."

"Peggy, I wouldn't exactly call him a criminal," Tracey began, hoping that her explanation would calm the girl. "If he were, he wouldn't have had the option of working for us instead of serving a sentence."

"He is *serving a sentence*," the girl declared, emphasizing the legal term. "He has to work here for six months, full time. If he doesn't, he has to go to jail. That makes him a criminal."

"He's gotten into trouble," Tracey amended firmly. "And it was the first time. There's a special program in this county in which we try to have first-time offenders do community service work instead of going to prison, where they'll meet hardened criminals."

"Well, it's better for them to meet hardened criminals than innocent, unsuspecting citizens!" Peggy retorted peevishly. "I had no idea when I applied to do my internship here that I'd be associating with people like that!"

Tracey thought of the enthusiasm in Cody's voice

when he'd talked about Maqu, and the light in his brown eyes when she'd observed him a few minutes earlier. "People like what, Peggy?"

The girl stared at her, wide-eyed, unable to believe that Tracey had asked the question again. "Why . . . why, you know—people who are . . . dangerous."

"Peggy, I really don't think Cody is dangerous. I've read the records of his case, and I think this was an unfortunate happening, not a pattern of behavior for him."

"You don't *know* that."

"No, but I trust him, and more important, the judge trusts him. If he'd thought Cody was a threat to anyone, he wouldn't have made him a part of this community service program."

"Lots of judges have made mistakes," Peggy shot back. "The newspapers are full of stories about people out on bail or on parole who commit other crimes." She stood up impatiently. "I'm going to write to the director of my summer school and to the liaison officer at Easton who coordinates these internships. They need to know about this so they won't send anyone else to Southwest to work."

"Peggy, has Cody bothered you in any way?" Tracey asked the question calmly, although she was beginning to seethe inside. "Has he touched you or threatened you or said something that offended you?"

Startled, Peggy hesitated, but only for a moment. "No, but that isn't the point. I simply don't want to be associated with that type of person." Her expressive eyes gleamed angrily. "Come on, be realistic, Tracey!"

Those words made Tracey's anger come to a boil. First Davis and now this . . . spoiled brat of a girl! What was he doing, anyway, telling the whole world that she was living in a fantasy?

Peggy was going on angrily. "I can't believe you're taking this attitude. I expected you to tell me that you'd take him off the guide staff and send him to jail where he belongs and stop this stupid 'young felons program' or whatever it was that Madeleine called it."

"I can't do that, Peggy," Tracey replied, trying to keep her voice level when she wanted to yell at the girl instead. "He's doing a good job and obeying all our rules. And I don't want to stop the program. I believe in it; I think it can do a lot of good."

"Oh? Well, what about the harm it can do if he suddenly stops obeying the rules?" Peggy demanded. She stood up, impatience and anger in every line of her body. "I'm going to do something about this, Tracey. I don't intend to have my summer ruined!"

Tracey stood to face her, trying to be calm and at the same time think of something completely infuriating to say. "Peggy, think it over before you write any letters or do anything to cause a lot of turmoil," she said coldly. Then she added sarcastically, "Why, who knows? A few days from now you and Cody may be the best of friends."

"I doubt that," Peggy snapped. She turned abruptly and started to walk away; then she stopped. She turned back dramatically to look at Tracey, her green eyes blazing. "If you won't listen to reason, I'm going to talk to Davis about this. He'll take care of it."

Peggy walked away very fast, and Tracey sat back down on the bench. So her impulsive decision to put Cody on the guide staff *was* going to cause trouble after all. Davis was bound to be upset, since Peggy was in such a state, and he'd be sure to take this as more evidence that Tracey wasn't facing facts. He wasn't taking her abilities seriously at all, and if things kept building up and building up, she could eventually lose her job.

Suddenly the afternoon wasn't nearly so beautiful as it had been, and all the excitement Tracey had been feeling about her animals turned to frustration and anger. Peggy was the one she should have put in the kitchen! She could have chopped up vegetables and fruits all summer long and never even known that Cody existed.

Chapter Five

Just the faintest light was filtering into Tracey's bedroom when she woke the next day, and the air drifting through her open window was sharply cool with the early morning. She stretched, then pushed the pillow up under her head, sleepily surveying the cream-colored walls of the little room, watching the breeze move the matching curtains. This house was perfect for her, she thought for the dozenth time. If everything worked out and she stayed at Southwest permanently, maybe she'd buy it.

If everything worked out . . . Her brain came awake. She couldn't wait for things to work themselves out. Today she had to do something about the problem with Peggy and Cody. She had to keep Cody at Southwest and prevent Peggy from complaining to her college and to the media.

She only wished that she could keep her from complaining to Davis, but there was faint hope of that. The only thing she could do was invite him to her office sometime that day and explain that Peggy was not about to be attacked by a maniac every time she came to work.

The idea of seeing him made her shiver a little, and she pulled the sheet up over her shoulders. Her campaign to put him into the proper perspective obviously wasn't working.

Drowsily she let in the memories she'd been keeping at bay: the sound of his voice saying, "I'll see you, Tracey"; the light brush of his hand on her arm as he spoke. Oh, his hands . . .

She closed her eyes and let herself drift. Every touch came floating back to tantalize her senses: his hand enclosing hers the day they met; his arm grazing hers as they walked out to her car after the board meeting; his fingers on the sensitive skin of her wrist.

Then the telephone beside her bed began to ring, and she knew before she answered that the voice on the other end would be his.

"Tracey?"

It wasn't fair. His calling when she had just been dreaming about him was too much. She wasn't strong enough to deal with this.

"Yes." The word was just above a whisper.

"It's Davis Turnbo. I'm sorry to call so early, but I've got a hell of a day ahead, and I didn't know when I'd get another chance. Can you have dinner with me tonight?"

Dinner! She was psyching herself up just to get through a business appointment with him, not a whole evening. She didn't know how she could have him in her office for twenty minutes; she certainly couldn't go out to dinner with him.

"Davis, I can't." She was surprised that her voice sounded crisp and pleasantly businesslike. "Why don't you come to my office sometime today or tomorrow?"

"Because tomorrow's going to be just like today, and so are all the rest of the days this week. I've just acquired a new construction company, and it's going to eat up my time for a week or two until I get it straightened out."

"Then maybe we could wait until after that."

"No, we can't." Impatience crept into his tone. "There's a problem with Peggy. I called Gerald yesterday, and he said you were the one making the decisions about the temporary help, so I need to see you. This is something that has to be taken care of right now. I'm trying to talk Peggy out of going to the media; at this stage Southwest certainly doesn't need any bad publicity."

He was insistent, sure of himself, accustomed to getting his own way, and that certitude vibrated through the instrument in her hand. He was a hard person to say no to.

"But, Davis . . ."

"Fine, then, it's settled. I'll pick you up at 7:00, and we'll drive out to The Territorial Station. See you then."

He hung up before she had a chance to protest, and

she lay propped up on one elbow, the receiver still in her hand. She replaced it slowly, berating herself for not being forceful enough to refuse. Why hadn't she lied and said she had another date for tonight that she couldn't possibly break?

She threw back the covers and got up. She'd go in to work early, she decided. She'd stay very busy all day, and the evening would be nothing but her last appointment for the day.

But The Territorial Station wasn't exactly part of a typical workday. And neither was Davis Turnbo.

Davis left the Mercedes at the end of Tracey's flagstone walk and got out of it brusquely. She'd better be ready, he thought. That stack of papers on his desk at home would still be there at midnight unless he got to them before then, and they had to be read and signed tonight.

But he'd probably be home plenty early enough, he told himself as he raised the knocker and let it fall. No matter how strong his attraction was to her wide amber eyes and passionate intensity, he wasn't going to give in to it. It wouldn't be any good for either of them; they'd already proved that they couldn't even communicate.

He moved restlessly to reach for the knocker once more. No, all they needed to do was get something worked out about Peggy and that guy on parole or whatever it was. They'd settle that over dinner and make it an early evening.

The door opened under his hand. She stood just inside it in a sea green dress. It outlined every curve of her body against the pale background of the walls and made his fingers ache to touch her creamy skin through the openwork pattern of its crocheted fabric. Her shoulders were completely bare; a band around the neck held the dress up over the softness of her high, round breasts.

"Hello, Davis."

Slowly, almost reluctantly, his eyes moved up to hers. "Hello, Tracey."

He helped her into the car and drove back out to the main road. He said very little, and she couldn't seem to think of a topic that would draw him out. She made remarks about two or three different subjects, but he responded to each of them with only a few words.

She shifted in her seat and shook her hair back to look at him. The contours of his face were thoughtfully still, and the lowering sun was glinting off his mustache in a veritable portrait of serenity. But that picture was a lie—the long lines of his body held an unaccountable tautness. He was sitting casually, apparently relaxed, controlling the wheel with only one big hand, but a throbbing tension was just underneath the surface.

He turned out onto the highway for the long drive to the secluded restaurant, and she tried again. "So you've bought a new company? Are you going to run it yourself?"

"Just for a while. I always do all the decision making myself with a new business until I get it straightened out financially." He glanced at her as he spoke, his eyes unreadable, shaded by heavy lids and thick lashes.

She waited for him to go on, but he didn't, and she

watched his profile, clean and hard against the orange glow that was the beginning of the sunset. His eyes were fastened on the road, and his lips were settled into an almost sullen arch.

Indignant, she looked away, staring into the infinite distance where the plain stretched toward the mountains. He seemed on the verge of being angry with her—and all this had been his idea in the first place!

Then, as if he sensed her feelings and realized that he was being rude, he turned to her. "Tracey . . ."

She lifted her eyes to his. He smiled, and heat moved across her as if he had reached out and put his hand on her bare skin.

"I'm sorry, Tracey," he apologized. "I've got too much on my mind."

She felt her lips curve in an answering smile, but frustration tore at her. Why did it have to be this way? He had too much on his mind; she had too much on hers. They were going out to talk and try to solve one of those problems. Why couldn't everything be different? Why couldn't they be going out just because they wanted to be together?

He tried to make up for his silence by beginning to entertain her. He told her more about his new company, and he asked about her day. He inquired about the baby spider monkeys she'd talked about to him and Peggy when they'd met at the snack bar, and he teased her about Maqu. They laughed again about the rhino's attempted charge of the Jeep, and the tension began to dissipate at last. By the time they pulled into the parking lot at the restaurant, she had almost forgotten why they had come. It was almost as if he really did want nothing but to be with her.

The maitre d' met them as they entered the restaurant, which was luxuriously decorated in turn-of-the-century style. Tracey looked around the foyer with delight; the mirrors and drapes, the chandeliers and flocked wallpaper, made the entire place seem to be a holdover from the Gay Nineties.

Then Davis put his hand on the small of her back as the maitre d' turned to lead them to their table, and she no longer cared what the room looked like or where she was. The thin fabric of her dress did nothing to keep his warmth away from her, and its open pattern let his fingertips graze her bare skin.

She had a wild desire to lean back against his long hard body and turn into his arms, right in the middle of the diners sitting around the demurely white-clothed tables. She remembered exactly how his body had felt pressed against hers, and his hand on the sensitive skin of her back was making her want it again.

At last they reached the table, situated in a private corner near the back of the room, and she slid gratefully into the red velvet covered armchair that he held for her. He sat down opposite her, and while he consulted with the waiter about the wine she picked up the menu and pretended to study it.

She stared blindly at the elegant black script against the glossy white paper and tried to think. This wasn't a date; she had to remember that. He had brought her here because he was concerned about Peggy. They were here to talk business.

But her body couldn't seem to realize that, and it was a terrible struggle to fight down this magnetic attraction that he held for her. Restlessly she fingered the crisp white napkin at her place. As soon as they ordered, she decided, she would bring up the subject of Peggy and Cody. They could discuss the problem over dinner and then go straight home. She had to get away from him as quickly as she could.

Davis glanced around the room; then his eyes came back to rest on her. "This is the perfect place for you," he told her, smiling. "Sitting in that armchair in your high-necked dress, you look as if you would have fit right into Arizona Territory."

She smiled back at him, and the expression in his eyes brought a sudden flush into her cheeks. She looked away and surveyed the room as he had done, searching for a distraction.

She concentrated on the reflection of the crystal chandeliers in the polished pine ceiling, and the enormous gilt-framed mirrors and paintings. The drapes were heavy red velvet to match the chairs; the thick carpet was red, discreetly patterned in black.

"I've heard so much about this place since I moved out here," she told him. "And it does live up to its billing." She chuckled. "But I don't know about the name. Do you think that things really looked like this in territorial days?"

"Could have," he answered as the waiter brought the wine. "After all, lots of luxuries reached the territory before statehood did. We were one of the last states to be admitted to the Union."

He poured for them both. "I can't speak from personal experience about territorial days, but I do know that this restaurant hasn't changed in years." He took a sip of the wine. "When I was a kid it looked like heaven to me." He smiled and shook his head at the memory.

"Did your family come to dinner here often?"

He raised an eyebrow at the idea. "Oh, no, there was no way we could've afforded that. I came here once with my uncle, who was a carpenter doing some repair work in the kitchen. I wandered into the dining room and just looked around for what seemed like hours. Even with no one in here it was the most fascinating place I'd ever been."

She smiled back. "I can understand that. When I was a kid we lived so far out in the country that I'd have been thrilled to go out for a hamburger, much less to a place like this." She took a sip of the wine. "Did you have a big family?"

He nodded. "Two brothers, one sister, three sets of aunts and uncles, and cousins always around. Did you?"

"No. I'm an only child, and my parents were killed in an accident when I was very young. I was raised by an aunt and uncle on a small farm in Iowa. I used to dream about a life like yours, with brothers and sisters and other children around all the time."

He nodded thoughtfully. "It was fun, but it wasn't all wonderful. We always needed more than we had of everything: more money, more space, once in a while more food, even. I was the oldest and I tried to help, tried to see that the younger kids had a few of the things they needed. My dad just never understood how to make money, or how to manage it. All he ever had was that small ranch, and he was right on the verge of losing it when he died."

"Is it the ranch you have now?"

"It was the beginning of it. I bought it from my brothers and sisters after Dad died, and then I added surrounding land as I could afford it."

"Then you were grown when he died."

"Yes. I already had my first two companies."

"Did you go back to live on the ranch right then?"

"No. I hired a manager and started trying to make it pay again. That's what I love about my businesses: the challenge of making each company become independent and self-supporting."

"Like Southwest?" she asked with feigned innocence, unable to resist.

He shrugged and made a wry face. "Like Southwest," he agreed. "I know you think I act as if it's solely my property, but it *has* to become a paying proposition, at least partially. I know how to do that."

"But some of the rest of us have ideas that need to be recognized, too," she told him as the waiter appeared to take their order for dinner. "There are things just as important as the balance sheet, you know."

He held up one finger, as if to say he'd challenge that in a moment, and they ordered. Once the man was gone he said, "Nothing else is as important. If I learned anything from my childhood, it's that your finances have to be in order before anything else can be right."

She shook her head, staring into the blue of his eyes. "That's not always true—there were no financial problems in my childhood, but everything else was awful."

He absorbed that, and then he nodded, a reluctant gesture of agreement. "I guess I just like to concentrate on the money angle of any situation. . . ." He hesitated, twirling the stem of his glass between his fingers, then went on thoughtfully. "Maybe because I don't know what to do about anything else."

The pain that she'd seen in his eyes before was suddenly there again, darkening them to the color of smoke, and the openness that had been growing between them disappeared in that instant. Instinctively she knew that he wasn't talking about Southwest anymore, or even about business at all.

They were silent for a few minutes, his eyes on the middle distance, while he retreated into that private world he'd been in at the beginning of the evening. He held the glass up, but he didn't take a drink; he pressed it thoughtfully, with unconscious sensuality, against his lips, and she had trouble looking away from them.

For a moment she hesitated, wanting to reach out to him, to question him, to help him with the hurting memories. But his face was hard, completely closed to her. He was a stranger all over again.

She took a sip of her wine, watching the light play on the pale liquid as she set the glass down. She'd stick to her resolve—they didn't need to get more involved with each other. They needed to discuss the problem that had brought them there and leave.

"Is Peggy still upset about working with Cody Howard?"

He didn't answer for a minute, and she glanced back at him. His eyes were on her face, but his thoughts were miles away.

"Davis?"

"Yes?"

"Has Peggy calmed down?"

Then the look was gone and he was alert again, guarded, as he took a drink of the wine. He put his mind to the question. "Not a whole lot. And she won't until Cody's reassigned or removed from Southwest," he said crisply. "I'm not so sure that this young felon program was such a good idea after all. I told Gerald it might be better just to drop it entirely."

"Oh, no!" Gerald had mentioned that, but somehow she hadn't taken it seriously. She'd assumed the worst would be that Cody would have to be taken off the guide staff, not that he could actually be sent to some other institution, or, failing that, even to jail.

She looked up at Davis, frowning with worry. "But I don't want us to drop the program," she protested. "I think it can do a lot of good. It's the kind of alternative we've needed in this country for a long time for young people in trouble."

"Yes, but we have to think about the young people who aren't in trouble," he answered firmly, as if he'd given the matter a lot of thought. "It doesn't make sense to have them scared silly. I suggested to Peggy that she simply ask for a different partner, but she refuses to go to staff meetings with Cody, or be associated with him at all."

"I'm sorry Peggy's taking this attitude," she replied. "I don't think she has any reason to be afraid of Cody. I think he's just a nice guy who's had a bad break."

"Well, I hope you're right. But before this goes any farther, I intend to make sure. Peggy's my responsibility for the summer, and I'm going to take care of her."

"Your responsibility?"

"Yes. John Smalley is one of the best friends I've ever had, and he's too old and feeble to know what's going on with his granddaughter. Peggy's dad, John's son, asked me to look out for her while she's here, and I have to make sure she's safe."

"I really think she is." She spoke calmly, but an unreasoning relief flooded her veins, and her hand shook as she picked up her glass. He wasn't interested in Peggy romantically; he was an old friend of her family!

"Because your instinct tells you he's harmless," he mused. "Is that why you assigned him to the guide staff instead of to something behind the scenes?"

She nodded and sipped her wine. "Yes, that and the fact that he can do us a lot of good as a guide. He's really interested in the animals and excited about them."

"But if he's a dangerous type, he doesn't need to be there."

"The judge would have sent him to prison if *he'd*

considered Cody dangerous, and my impression agrees with his." She played with the edge of the starched white napkin, her wide eyes holding his. "Look, Davis, I think Peggy's overreacting a little. I think Cody's a kid from a poor background, one who hasn't had very many advantages, but not one who's out to get revenge on the world. He uses his streetwise charm to survive, and it's obvious that he doesn't trust most people too much, but he has a vulnerability about him, almost a sweetness. He's not about to attack Peggy."

His eyes bored into hers, as if her words had struck a familiar chord. "I'd like to meet him and judge for myself," he decided. "But, Tracey, even if I agree with you, I don't think Peggy's ever going to be comfortable working with him."

She shrugged. "Perhaps not. But I really hate to move him away from the guide staff now that he's just getting into it." She looked at him pleadingly, everything forgotten now but Cody. "Davis, I wish you *would* meet him. You'll like him. He can make a good life for himself if he's given half a chance, and we're in the position to give him that chance."

He nodded, considering. "Is he from around here?"

"Tucson. He's finished high school, and he's held several jobs. Construction and things like that. In fact, he was working when he was arrested, and this conviction cost him that job."

"He was in a fight in some bar, wasn't he?"

"Yes." She was surprised that he knew that, and suddenly she wondered what else he already knew about the entire situation. "My guess is that he had quite a lot of provocation," she went on. "The man he fought with is fairly prominent socially, I hear, and I think there was some discussion about which side of the tracks Cody was from and that kind of thing."

Davis inclined his head abruptly. "The other man involved was Richard Barnes. I've known him for a long time." He took a sip of wine. "I'll meet Cody," he said. "I'll make time to bring Peggy to work tomorrow, and I'll talk to him then."

The poached fillets of sole arrived then, and as Tracey tasted the cold herbed sauce that blanketed them, she felt his eyes on her. She looked up to meet his gaze, and it told her that he was no longer interested in Cody, nor in Peggy; his food was untouched in front of him.

"I said you looked like someone out of territorial days," he told her, as if that conversation had never been interrupted, "but since then I've decided that that can't be true. There are too many things about that dress that are strictly up to date." His blue gaze followed the curve of her shoulders and then dropped to linger on her breasts.

Her nipples sprang to life as if he had touched them, and she thrilled with the sensation. What would it be like if his hands? . . . Her eyes went to his lips.

Then she shook her hair around her face and bent her head to concentrate on her food. Silently she made another decision. When he took her home she would leave him at the door. The magnetism he exuded was too potent for her to handle. She wasn't going to touch him, or let him kiss her again.

But when they left the restaurant he pulled her arm through his, and the weakness that flashed through her combined with the magnificent night to mock her resolve. She didn't have the strength to take her arm away, and they walked slowly, very close together, their arms touching, their thighs and hips brushing lightly as they moved. The desert night stretched all around them, and as they strolled across the lushly landscaped parking area she let him twine her fingers into his.

The air had changed from when they went inside; it was cooler, and it carried the freshness of open country. It was almost intoxicating—the sense of liberation in the great space, the wine she had drunk, the mysterious closeness that had woven itself between them again as they talked.

His fingers let go of hers reluctantly as she slid into the deep leather seat of the Mercedes. The gesture was so provocative, so tantalizing, that her breath caught in her throat, and when he had walked around and gotten in behind the wheel she couldn't take her eyes off his bold profile outlined against the night.

He opened the roof on the car to the spaciousness of the sky, and she leaned back into the softness of the seat, welcoming the breeze that played in her hair. She made an attempt to watch the palely lit landscape as it slipped by them, but her gaze came back to his face every time she tried to take it away.

He felt it, and he glanced away from the road to

smile at her. "You said you'd wanted a childhood like mine," he remarked. "Were you terribly unhappy?"

The sudden reference to that painful time made her tense, and he sensed it. His eyes left the road again for a second to touch hers briefly, as if to say that he understood.

"Sometimes," she admitted. "There were no other children for miles around, and none of the adults—my aunt, my uncle and the hired hand—ever had more than a couple of minutes a day to devote to me." She shrugged. "But I guess it was good for me. I certainly learned to cope with loneliness and to amuse myself."

"Did you have any pets?"

"Lots. In fact the animals on the farm were my salvation. I made them my friends, and I spent hours taking care of them and learning how to handle them. When I first heard about zoos and wild animal preserves I knew right then that that was the kind of work I wanted to do."

"And now that you're doing it, does it make you happy?"

"Very. I can get so involved that I forget everything else exists."

"Is that what happiness means, do you think? Having work or a hobby or something that you can lose yourself in?" His tone was casual, but there was an underlying earnestness in it.

"Well, maybe it is for me," she said, seriously considering his question. "But who knows what it is for someone else? I suppose everyone has to find his own way to be happy."

"And some don't find it," he remarked cryptically. "Maybe because of the other people in their lives."

"Maybe, but I don't think—"

"Oh, forget it," he interrupted gruffly. Then, as if he realized how brusque he'd sounded, he added in a lighter tone, "We'll solve the problems of the world another time, okay? Let's not try to do it all tonight."

He concentrated on the road, and they drove in silence for a few minutes. Then his eyes met hers again. His face was shadowed, his sideways glance heavy and enigmatic, but she saw the desire in his eyes as clearly as if the sun had been shining.

The bright flash of wanting that was carried in that look, the radiant magnetic message of it, lanced into her and illuminated every cell in her body. Neither of them spoke; it was as if they had an innate agreement to which words were entirely alien. She felt her cheeks flame, and as he turned away to look back out through the windshield, she held her face up to the freshness of the air coming through the roof.

It didn't cool her, though, and her pulse thudded unevenly as the car slid through the darkness.

She didn't look directly at him again until they had reached her house and he had parked in the little graveled semicircle at the foot of her front walk. Then he opened the door on her side of the car, and she looked up into his face to find that same seductive intentness that she'd seen before.

She couldn't get into this; she had to break the spell. "I had a really good time," she told him lightly.

"So did I, and I hope you'll go out with me again sometime," he answered quickly, falling in with her mood. His tone was as easy as hers, and he didn't touch her as they climbed the curving tiled steps and walked up the flagstone path between the golden poppies and yuccas she had planted there. "Maybe next time we can go to a place where there's dancing, too," he went on as they reached the door.

She nodded. "Maybe so. If we manage to solve this problem with our children, we'll have a reason to go out and celebrate."

He chuckled, a deep, rich sound that rippled over her skin like a caress. "Well, you may be old enough to be Cody's mother, but I certainly couldn't be Peggy's father. After all, I'm only twenty-one, myself."

She laughed. "It's a relief to know that. At least it was legal for you to order the wine tonight."

His smile was his only answer, and in the light that the moon was spilling across the porch his eyes glimmered with wanting her.

Then he touched her. He traced the shape of her cheek in a movement so light and ethereal that it seemed impossible for his big hand to execute. His fingers were pleasantly rough, and their slight abrasiveness stirred every nerve ending in her body to fascinated life.

He continued to trace a path down her throat until he reached the barrier of thin fabric around her neck; then he followed the edge of it to find the curve of her shoulder.

His other hand found the bare skin of her back, and as it trailed along her spine the contact galvanized her. He urged her toward him with the gentlest of pressures, and she drew in a deep, helpless breath because suddenly his lips were where his fingers had been— feathering along her collarbone and coming back to the hollow of her throat.

She leaned into the warmth of his mouth with a movement dictated by her instincts, not her mind. She was no longer a rational being; she was entirely flesh and blood, trembling desires and empty senses waiting to be filled.

"Davis . . ." she whispered into his hair. She felt her lips move, but she was hardly aware that she spoke. It was as if his name were a natural part of her breathing, as if he were now an integral facet of her life.

He didn't answer. His lips were progressing relentlessly up the curve of her throat, and they kept on until they reached the edge of her mouth. Then they stopped, and her breath stopped with them. Time and the world stopped, too, and nothing moved in the still paleness of the moonlight.

His hand spread with ultimate sureness over her back, then slid up over her nape to tangle in her hair. He tilted her head back at just the right angle, then gently, delicately, his lips began to caress the contours of her mouth. They traveled around the edge of it, then they settled at one corner and she felt the flashing thrill of the tip of his tongue as it began to search for hers.

Her lips fell open to him, and in that second the kiss

became an entirely different thing. His mouth captured hers with all the hunger that was pent up in him, and with every stroke of his tongue against hers, and every thrust that it made into the softness of her mouth, he took possession of her body and her mind.

His other hand was just under her breast, and as his mouth took hers it moved up to claim the soft mound. Without a thought she leaned into his embrace, the taut tip of her breast begging for the delight of his touch, her body coming to him as naturally as her lips had done.

His fingers found the swollen nipple and teased it between them for a moment. Desire sang in her veins and pulsed to the very core of her being.

Then both his hands were laced into the masses of her hair, cradling her head in their powerful grip, and his mouth filled hers with such ecstasy that she lost all sense of time and place. She knew nothing except that she wanted him; she wanted his hands on her skin and his body on hers.

He was drowning in the honey of her mouth, and passion was pulsing through him in a pounding rhythm. Her arms slipped around him, and one of her hands teased his ear, tantalizing its way down the side of his neck with a gossamer caress that took his breath away. Finally he pulled back to look into her face.

Her eyes were half-closed under their heavy veil of dark lashes, but as soon as his lips left hers she opened them in silent protest. They were glowing with the fervor of the kiss, as sensuously alluring as they always were to him. Even in the uncertain glow cast by the porch light and the weak moon he could see their exotic color and their vivid gleam.

Feelings ran so strong in her, so wild, so close to the surface. That drew him to her with a force that he could not resist.

But he had to resist it. Pain would run as deep in Tracey as passion did; there was something so poignant in her, so vulnerable. And he might not be able to make her happy. He'd failed Marla without knowing how or why, and he couldn't take that risk again.

As he continued to look at her every nerve in his body tingled in alarm. If they got involved, it wouldn't be one of the casual liaisons which were all he had allowed himself during the past five years. His first instinct had been right. This woman would be different. And it couldn't be right for either of them.

His hands fell to his sides, and he stepped away from her.

"Tracey, I have to go." His voice was rough, almost harsh, discordant in the quiet. "Good night."

The tone shook her, and she tilted her head to look up at him, but the words hardly registered at first. Her mind was still dormant; she was aware only of her protesting body. It was screaming that he'd taken his hands away, that they were no longer touching.

He left her then, turning on the heel of his boot and walking rapidly back to the car while she was still realizing what he'd said.

Shocked, she stood looking after him. What was he doing? Why had he changed so rapidly? It was almost as if she had made him angry, but she had no idea what she'd done. What had happened to him?

Dazed and hurt, she turned and stumbled into the darkness of the house. For a while she wandered through it without turning on any lights, her mind and her body a chaos of hurt and frustration, embarrassment and wondering.

But no matter how she tried she couldn't understand, so at last she went to her room and undressed. She washed her face and found her nightgown and turned back her bed without once thinking about a single thing she was doing. Then she stumbled barefoot over the polished board floors of the house and out onto the painted cement one of the back patio.

Geoffrey got up from his sleep and rambled over to join her as she settled herself into the padded cushions of a redwood lawn chair, but the pats she gave him were less than perfunctory, and he soon went back to his bed.

The moon was a pale sphere floating high in the cloudless sky, and the light it shed was becoming brighter by the minute. She watched it, her eyes so wide that she felt as if they would never close again.

She listened to the snuffling of Foxfire and Trampas, and to the incredible stillness of the spaces stretching far beyond. She smiled wryly to herself. *She* was the one who was threatened; Davis was far more dangerous to her than Cody would ever be to Peggy.

She breathed in the air and the smells of the desert, and ran her tongue over her lips; she could still taste the nectar of his kiss. Every nerve in her body was alert and awake; her senses were so acute that she was sure she would never be able to quiet them again.

And she would never be able to sleep again. So she sat with her legs drawn up against the dry chill of the night, her arms around her knees, until the moon began to set and the hour before dawn fell around her like thick, dark velvet.

Chapter Six

By Friday morning Tracey was resigned to the fact that she would have to change Cody's assignment. Davis hadn't called to say that he'd persuaded Peggy to change her mind—or to say anything at all—and Gerald *had* called, twice, in fact, to say that Peggy was complaining to the officials at Easton and that he was certain that her next calls would be to the media.

He was so worried about the possible damage to Southwest's image that Tracey finally told him that she'd move Cody to a less visible job; it was the quickest way to quiet things down. There simply wasn't time to let Cody prove himself.

Now, on her way across the zoo to meet Cody at the nursery, she tried to think how to break the news to him. She just hoped that he wouldn't be so disappointed that he would lose all the enthusiasm he'd brought with him to Southwest.

When she arrived he was already there, wandering around outside the glass-walled display room.

"Hi, Cody. Am I late?"

"No. I finished my first tour a little early, so I came on over." He was leaning against the glass window to the cage that held the two little spider monkeys, looking more relaxed than she'd ever seen him.

"Cody . . ." she began, then stopped.

He looked at her questioningly, the smile that had greeted her in his eyes as well as on his lips. He was different, more confident already; working at the zoo had been good for him.

She hesitated. She just couldn't tell him that he was no longer a guide. Not yet.

"Have you been inside the nursery today?" she asked at last.

"No."

"Well, there's a new addition I want you to meet."

They went inside, and LuAnn led them down the back hallway and into a room where the only occupant was a baby cougar.

"His name is Sand," she said. "We just got him yesterday from the Arizona-Sonora Desert Museum; they had a surplus of males."

Sand was crying and growling, putting up an awful fuss. Cody grinned at him.

"He's great," he pronounced. "But what's this with all the spots? He looks more like a leopard than a cougar."

"All baby cougars have them," Tracey explained. "They're camouflage for them in the wild. He'll lose them in a few months."

"I took him home with me last night to keep on trying to feed him," LuAnn said, "but he screamed so much I'm afraid to do it again. I might get thrown out of my apartment."

"Cody, he needs someone to feed him here in the nursery," Tracey said. "He really needs a lot of attention. He's hungry, but he doesn't associate a bottle with food and it's going to be a full-time job to teach him to eat."

Cody nodded to show that he was listening, but his eyes were still on Sand.

"Think you could handle that?" Tracey asked.

He turned to her, surprised and pleased. "You'd trust me with him?" His voice almost broke on the last word, and the expression on his face spoke volumes.

He swallowed hard as his eyes held hers, and the force of his emotions struck her like a blow. Good heavens! Hadn't anyone ever trusted him before? Had the whole world always put him down the way Richard Barnes had?

The beginning of tears pricked at her eyes. She nodded. "Yes, Cody, I trust you with him," she said with slow emphasis. "Do you want him?"

Wordlessly he nodded.

"You need to understand, though, that he'll be a full-time job for quite a while. You won't have time to take care of him and be a tour guide, too."

He nodded again, his eyes going back to the baby

cougar as if drawn by a magnet. "That's okay. I can't believe I'm really going to get to work with the animals!" His lips twisted in a wry grin, half-humorous and half-bitter. "I think I've always liked animals better than people."

There was something so young about the eagerness in his face, and something so very ancient about the resignation in his voice, that she reached out to touch his arm. "I hope there'll be at least one or two of us people at Southwest that you'll like almost as well as you like Sand," she said.

He chuckled. "It's possible, I guess," he said. "It's possible."

She laughed, too, as she glanced at LuAnn who was mouthing the words "He'll be great." Relief flooded through her. It was hard to believe that a problem she'd worried so much about had been solved so easily.

She touched his arm again, this time in good-bye. "Well, Cody, I need to run," she said. "You stay and let LuAnn give you instructions for becoming a surrogate parent, and I'll tell Madeleine about the change in your assignment."

He was holding out his hand to Sand, already absorbed in trying to make friends with him. "Right," he said.

The painless way the problem with Cody had worked itself out gave her a lift for the morning, but the rest of the day was hectic, as usual. When she arrived home that afternoon her only thought was to celebrate Friday and banish the entire week from existence, and with it the eternal wish that Davis would call her.

Every day since the evening they'd gone out she'd put in her usual long hours at the zoo, and each day when she finally did get home she'd ridden and worked with Foxfire in a more disciplined way than she had since she'd come to Southwest. She'd also cultivated the flower beds she'd planted when she first moved in to try to keep herself busy every second.

But each night, when she'd finally dropped, exhausted, into bed, Davis came to the forefront of her consciousness and stayed there. When she thought of him her lips still burned with the touch of his and her palms yearned to shape the contours of his chest and shoulders.

She'd tried to tell herself that it was simply sexual attraction that made her feel that way. It was just that he held a marvelous power that she'd never known existed; nothing about her relationship with Eric had even approached this wild longing that Davis awakened in her. Her body begged for him to call her.

But it was more than just a physical attraction, a small stubborn voice inside her always argued. He understood something about her that she hardly knew herself; he had given her a glimpse of something deep within her that she hadn't even known existed. And he'd done it before he'd ever touched her. There was something in his eyes.

Now it was Friday, and she didn't want to spend the whole weekend wishing that when her phone rang it would be Davis. He'd drawn away from her in the middle of a kiss and left without any explanation, and that was the end of that. She'd see him when she had to on business, and she'd try to forget as easily as he seemed to that there had ever been any kind of personal relationship between them.

She shrugged as she set up some jumps. It seemed that as far as he was concerned there *hadn't* been anything personal. A couple of casual kisses had meant nothing to him.

She concentrated on working Foxfire for a while; then she took the mare for a long ride, watching for the desert colors and the flowers that she loved—the red-tasseled ocotillo, the pink of the hedgehog cactus. She let the strong spell of the desert and the purple mountains in the far distance seep into her, and while she rode the entire perimeter of her rented acreage she soaked up the sun and the reflected heat from the earth. The warmth seemed to work in concert with the rhythm of the powerful animal moving under her to melt the tension out of her bones.

When the first hint of sunset streaked the sky she turned Foxfire back toward the stable. Once there, she dried and groomed the mare, then fed both her and Trampas, leaving them each with a bucket of oats and an affectionate pat.

Geoffrey was sitting expectantly beside his bowl when she got to the house, and she smiled at him as she took it into the kitchen to fill it. "Everybody's hungry around here," she said conversationally as she brought it back to him. "I'm beginning to think about supper myself."

She unfastened her belt and peeled the sweaty tail of her thin knit shirt away from her back; then she dropped wearily onto the chaise longue to slip out of her boots, knocking the dust from them and from her jeans.

Geoffrey stopped eating to growl. He stared at the corner of the house, on guard, but reluctant to leave his supper. Footsteps sounded on the stone walk that connected the back patio with the front porch, and she stood up, her boots in one hand.

Davis came into view, two large brown bags in his arms.

"No one answered my knock," he explained. "I thought you might be down at the stable."

She took off her hat, and when her hair tumbled from under it, she pushed it back from her face. "I was," she said finally. "I . . . I've been riding."

He grinned. "Looks like the horse won," he drawled, making a thorough inspection of her disheveled condition. "I had a feeling I should get over here right away."

Indignation flared in her. How could he appear on her doorstep smiling and teasing her like this after he'd walked away in the middle of a kiss?

She stared at him, not smiling back. "Oh, it really isn't as bad as it looks," she said coolly. "As soon as I have a shower and some dinner I'll be fine."

"Then your problems are solved," he announced briskly. "I have dinner right here in these bags, and I'll be more than happy to help you with your shower."

Color tinged her cheeks, and she didn't answer for a minute. Then an unwilling grin flitted across her lips. "Dinner is one thing, but about the shower . . ."

He laughed. "I know, I know. You'd like to get to know me better first. That's what they all say."

His tone was light and his words a continuation of the banter they'd shared on Tuesday night, but she sensed a weariness in him, a bone-tiredness. The fine white creases at the corners of his eyes seemed deeper, and although his dark tan summer suit was still crisp, he had loosened his tie and opened his collar.

He ran one hand distractedly through his hair. "I took a chance," he said, suddenly serious. "I didn't even take time to go home and change; I was afraid you'd go out." He glanced at the bundles in his arms. "I brought steaks and wine and stuff for a salad. Do you by any chance have two potatoes . . . and a free evening?" His blue gaze was hopeful, raw with need, and it went straight to her heart.

It was the first time she'd ever seen him not completely in control of a situation, and with a start she understood that that was because of her. He really wanted to be with her right now . . . he *needed* to be with her, and he wasn't sure that she wanted to be with him.

The realization hit her with an almost physical force, and suddenly she was glad that the chaise longue was still behind her. She'd been assuming that she hadn't crossed his mind since he'd left her, and that she'd never see him again. She'd been wrong.

At last she moved toward the kitchen door. "Come in, Davis. I'm not sure whether I have any potatoes, but I do have a free evening."

After they'd put the steaks and vegetables away she left him to build the mesquite fire in the grill on the patio and went to take her shower, glad for the chance to be alone for a few minutes. For a long while she stood under the hot spray, just trying to assimilate the fact that he was there.

Then she dried off quickly and took a strapless gauze sundress from her closet. She dressed quickly, slipping her feet into huaraches and arranging her wet hair into one thick braid down the middle of her back. She added some lip gloss and a touch of mascara, and then, on impulse, a long string of tiny turquoise chunks that matched the color of the dress.

When she came back into the kitchen he was opening the bottle of wine he'd brought. "I found the corkscrew, but you'll have to tell me where the glasses are."

He had taken off his coat and tie and rolled up his sleeves, and as he turned to greet her she saw that his pale blue shirt was open halfway down his chest. She stared at the blond hair curling against his bronzed skin. Her palms tingled, craving the feel of it.

His fingers tightened on the corkscrew, and his eyes swept her possessively. She was frozen there; she couldn't do anything else until they touched.

But they couldn't touch. Not when he might turn and walk away at any second.

Eventually she spoke, moving toward the cabinet at the end of the room. "They're up here, but I can't reach them unless I stand on a chair."

He came to her instantly, the length of his body

brushing hers as he reached for the shelf. He took two wineglasses down with an easy gesture, and as he handed them to her his bare forearm grazed hers.

"If you'll hold them, I'll pour," he said. "I thought we might as well have some wine while we work. After all, it's not easy to make a salad after a long, hard week."

He finished opening the bottle and poured the wine, then held his glass toward hers in a toast. "To Fridays," he said with an easy grin.

"To Fridays," she affirmed. They each took a sip of the fragrant wine. "Has it been a bad week?" she asked softly.

He shrugged. "You could say that. It's been frustrating. And exhausting." The words hung in the air for a moment, but instead of elaborating on them, he said, "I dropped by Southwest and met your friend, Cody."

"Oh? What did you think?"

"I liked him. Seems like a good kid to me." His sideways glance was keen. "You were right, Tracey. We might do some good with that young felons program."

"Did you tell Peggy that?"

"Yes, but it didn't do any good. She's already been calling around raising a fuss, and she can't back down now without losing face." He raised one eyebrow ruefully. "And, to be perfectly honest, I think she *is* a little bit scared of him. She'd get over it if she'd give him a chance, but . . ."

"I know. But I guess she won't get that chance. I changed Cody's assignment this morning."

"Where'd you put him?"

"We got a new baby cougar who needs a lot of care right now, so I gave the job to him. He's really happy about it." She sipped her wine. "Davis, he couldn't believe I'd trust him with that animal. Or with anything else, for that matter. I don't think we have any idea what his life so far has been like."

"Probably not. I doubt that either one of our childhoods can compare with his."

"Uh hmm," she agreed. "Or our present situations, either. At least *our* worst times are over."

Restlessly he set his glass down on the countertop. "I'll go check on the fire," he said abruptly. "You want to start the salad?"

There it was again: that sudden wall between them. She put the potatoes into the microwave oven and stood for a minute staring at its gleaming black face. Why was he there if all he wanted was to get away from her?

Finally the meat was done, the salad and potatoes were finished and the table was laid in her little dining alcove. He brought the sizzling steaks to the table as she was putting a large candle in the middle of it. He took the match from her and lit it as they sat down.

"You did a beautiful job on such short notice," he told her, indicating the attractively set table. "I'm really glad I dropped by."

The warm remark so close on the heels of his remoteness startled her. She'd never understand him, she thought helplessly.

"Well, I didn't do it all by myself," she answered lightly. "We did it together."

He put dressing on his salad. "And it's worked out about Peggy," he said in a relieved tone, as if that were something else they'd accomplished together. "She'll calm down now if she doesn't have to associate with Cody."

"I certainly hope so. We're losing a good guide by moving him. I was already getting calls from visitors saying how much they'd enjoyed his tours."

"But he'll do a good job with the cougar, too." He took a slice of fragrant garlic bread from the basket she held out to him. "It's been a problem, her being so hostile to him, but since I'm responsible for her this summer, in a way I'm glad."

Her eyes widened in surprise. "Why do you say that?"

He shrugged. "I was just thinking that it's better for her to feel this way than to be attracted to him. Then I'd *really* have trouble."

"I don't think I understand."

"Their backgrounds are so different, and that never works." He paused. "Well, that's a terrible generalization—I ought to say that it didn't work for me and my wife."

The words "my wife" stabbed her heart. "Your wife?"

"She was from an old, well-to-do family in Tucson, and I was from the other side of the tracks, like Cody. It was a disaster."

Automatically she put sour cream on her potato and salted and peppered it, but when she took a bite it was like cardboard in her mouth. Her mind was whirling, trying to take this in. He'd been married! Was his wife the reason he'd been so gruff that evening at the Mariposa when she'd mentioned his family?

She longed to ask what had happened to his marriage, but instead she said, "But your childhood can't mark you forever unless you let it. Your ranch isn't on the wrong side of the tracks now simply because it's yours."

He smiled bitterly. "Actually it's nowhere near the tracks at all. But Marla never lived there, so maybe she didn't realize that."

"Did you own the ranch then?"

"I had the land, but I built the house after she . . ." He stopped, then went on, forcing a lighter tone into his voice. "She hated the country; she had to be in town. We had a house in Tucson."

He was quiet for a minute, staring into the ruby-colored liquid in his glass. His eyes darkened until they were a hazy gray, and pain etched the tired lines deeper around his mouth.

Finally she spoke softly to distract him from the memories. "Do you like the country better?"

His eyes came back to hers, and after a minute he smiled. "Much. I'll never live in town again."

The sweet vulnerability in his smile drew an answering one from her, and immediately there seemed to be some sort of unspoken understanding between them and they relaxed. They began to eat hungrily, talking in a desultory way about her work. She told him about some of the people who had talked with her after her speech in Phoenix.

"Oh, that reminds me," he said. "I've been talking with Gerald about that donation from John and Diane Grant in Phoenix. The one they designated for a pair of snow leopards."

"I saw the letter about that," she said quickly, putting down her fork to give the subject her full attention. "And I'm so frustrated that they didn't just give us all that money with no strings attached. I could think of a dozen better ways to spend it."

"A pair of snow leopards will draw a lot of visitors," he said, and the tone of his voice reminded her of the remark he'd made about her living in a fantasy world where Southwest's finances were concerned.

"But there they'll be, just the two of them, all caged up," she answered tightly. "That amount of money ought to be used for the preserve."

He shrugged as if that point of view were of no importance at all, and resentment stung her. "Diane Grant thinks snow leopards are the most beautiful animals she's ever seen," he said. "So she wants some in an exhibit with her name on it. I don't see what's so wrong about that."

"She probably thinks they're so beautiful that she even has a coat made out of their skins," Tracey said scornfully.

Tension tightened his fingers on the handle of his fork. "You ought to be glad they gave the money, no matter what restrictions they put on it. Any addition to the zoo draws more visitors and creates interest that generates more donations."

Anger flared in her stomach. "Well, *you* ought to be

a little more discriminating," she retorted. "You and your generous friends need to wake up and come into the twentieth century." She couldn't resist adding sarcastically, "After all, we need to be realistic about this."

His lips thinned under his mustache, and his eyes darkened as they pierced hers. "It's too bad you're determined to be so unreasonable about it," he said. "I was hoping we'd be able to work together on this project without any problems."

"Work together?"

"Why, yes," he drawled, and his tone was a challenge. "Gerald insists that he isn't up to all the detailed planning meetings it'll take to get this under way."

"Well, then, wait until he is up to it," she snapped.

"We can't. The Grants want this done as soon as possible, and I can't really blame them."

"No doubt so as many visitors as possible will see the plaque with their name on it. Or is part of the money designated for a *monument* to hold their names?"

They stared at each other angrily for a minute, the ridiculous question hanging in the air between them, and then his lips began to curve in that irrepressible smile.

"As I remember, they stipulated Italian marble," he teased. "And the design is to be faintly reminiscent of the Lincoln Memorial."

They began to laugh together in sudden camaraderie, and the anger between them flowed away in the relaxing sound. They avoided the subject of the snow leopards and talked easily through the rest of the meal and that, added to the unexpected news that she would be seeing a great deal of him in the next few weeks, made her heart beat just a little faster.

When they had finished eating she stood up. "Let's take our wine into the living room," she said. "It's more comfortable in there."

He stood, too. "Tracey . . ."

The single candle guttered between them in the light breeze. It was the only light in the house; the last trace of the sun was fading away in the room's western window. But even in the dimness the desire in his eyes flared brightly, and its flames licked at every nerve in her body.

But they couldn't, she thought vaguely. She'd spent a week realizing that nothing personal would work between them. He could touch her, kiss her, melt everything in her until all she felt was mindless desire for him—and then not call her for days. And then he could suddenly appear on her patio with that irresistible question in his eyes.

She moved toward him without even realizing what she was doing, and he stepped around the table to meet her. They stood without touching, caressing each other with their eyes, and then his hand slipped around to fit the curve of her neck, tilting her face up to his.

His thumb moved in lazy circles, fondling the sensitive skin around her earlobe, and she heard the sound of her own indrawn breath, for a moment not even realizing what it was. His lips hovered above hers, almost touching them.

She didn't care anymore. It didn't matter how differ-

ent their opinions were, or how hard it was to understand him. She wanted him to keep his hands on her;
she wanted him to keep on caressing her bare skin; she
wanted his kiss. That was all she wanted in the whole
world.

His lips took hers, and the kiss was gentle for the
space of a pulsebeat; then it turned suddenly greedy.
His tongue tasted her lips first, then sampled the warm
recesses of her mouth with a hunger that took her
breath away.

"Tracey," he murmured against her mouth, "this is
what I wanted to do the other night." His voice was low
and rough with desire. "This is what I've wanted to do
ever since the first minute I saw you."

His eyelids were heavy with desire. She pulled back
to try to see up into his eyes, and his long fingers moved
slowly to the thick braid of her hair. He slid the clasp
off the end of it.

A small frisson of fear moved through her, an echo of
the alarm that had made her twist out of his arms the
first time he'd kissed her. It came hot on the heels of
the waves of desire that were beginning to build as they
had that night, waves that threatened to obliterate her
panic even as they created it. Her decision to live only
for the moment wavered. She couldn't do this, she
thought hopelessly; he had haunted her mind after one
kiss. If they made love, he would obsess her.

But she waited, very still, drowning in the blue
depths of his eyes.

Slowly, carefully, using both hands, he began to
loosen her hair, unwinding each twist of it with deliber-

ate purpose. He smoothed it once when he had finished; then, as if he couldn't wait, he plunged his fingers into the heavy mass of it with such wanton pleasure that she moaned with delight.

She reached for him with both arms, sliding them around his neck and pulling him to her with a hunger as intense as his. His shirt was smooth and cool against the bare skin of her upper arms, but the rock-hardness of his chest was warm and tantalizing. She pressed the softness of her breasts against it, reveling in the crispness of his curling hairs as they made contact with her skin.

Instinctively, pushing her thoughts away, she ran her tongue along his lips to tempt him even closer; he stopped the delicious torture by melding her mouth totally against his.

His tongue began an onslaught of stroking and touching, and she welcomed it, moving her own in rhythm with his until she couldn't breathe or think.

His hand moved down over the thin gauze of her dress to define her small waist and rounded hips; then it returned to her bare back and shoulders with a sensuous confidence so erotic that a passionate thrill raced through her.

She *didn't* care, she thought wildly. Even if making love with him would seal him into her consciousness forever, even if it would later break her heart, she wanted this. She wanted this to remember.

His rough fingers traced the line of her backbone; then his hand cupped her hips and pressed her to him. She felt the swelling of his passion, and she tangled her fingers into his hair and stood on tip-toe to shape herself to him.

He pressed her even closer and slowed the thrusting of their tongues. The rhythm of their kiss became leisurely, measured, but much more enticing, so seductive that they could no longer ignore its message.

Without interrupting the cadence of the kiss, without letting a modicum of space come between them, he swept her up into his arms and carried her into the dimness of the living room.

She was hardly aware that she was moving physically; emotionally she had been floating in an all new world since the beginning of his kiss. When his lips left hers at last, and he lowered her onto the wide couch, she had no idea where she was until she felt the rough weave of the white Haitian cotton against her skin. She sank into it, her eyes closed, filled with being so close to him. She didn't care whether she ever moved again. She had found something that she'd been needing all her life, a oneness of being that pierced her soul.

A long minute went by without his touch, and she opened her eyes. "Davis?" she whispered.

He was kneeling beside her, his hands on the pillow on either side of her. His eyes were very dark in the dim half-light, their lids heavy with desire. They were caressing her as passionately as his lips had just done.

His mouth curved in a lazy, sexy smile as his eyes met hers. Then slowly, deliberately, with movements as beguiling as his look, he pulled the elasticized top of her dress down and away from her firm breasts. Their ivory softness caught the light from the window; his tanned hand looked very dark against them as he cupped the fullness first of one and then the other, stroking the rosy tips with his thumb.

Then he bent his head and took one nipple into his mouth, holding it gently between his teeth and tongue. The purest pleasure she had ever known shot through her and sparkled along every vein in her body. He began to nip at her breast softly, to tease and fondle it, and all her doubts and fears were erased in the flood of excitement that washed through her.

She arched up to him and reached for him, pulling the back of his shirt out of his waistband. She ran her hands up under it and over the muscular contours of his back, whispering his name. For a long, long minute she was aware of nothing but his skin and his mouth and the fire that they were sending through her body. Then the balmy air from the open window struck her skin, and she realized that he'd removed her dress completely.

She grasped the buttons on his shirt and undid them, moving her hands to run her palms through the thick mat of hair on his chest, over the curves of his muscles, as she had wanted to do since the first time he had kissed her. She breathed a deep, ragged sigh as the satisfaction of that caress at first relieved, then heightened, the desires raging through her.

She tangled her fingers in his hair; then she found his flat nipples and teased them.

He gasped and shrugged out of his shirt without straightening, his hands coming back immediately to cup her breasts from the sides. The tiny turquoise pieces bit into her sensitized skin as the necklace fell into the valley between them.

Impatiently he looped it over her head and lowered his mouth to begin blazing a trail of kisses from the tip of one of her breasts to the other, lingering to bring each one to a pinnacle of excitement. She cried out as the incredible sensations penetrated to the very center of her being, and arched up to him again as his tongue and his lips pressed hot between them and began to move down over her flat stomach to the barrier of her lacy underwear.

Then that, too, was gone, and in moments he was naked on the couch beside her. She ran her hands over him greedily, trying to learn every inch of him while he was with her, while the magic that was in his hands and his lips was bringing every nerve in her body to quivering life. She explored and caressed him; she held him and pressed her fingers into his flesh, learning it, marking it, making it hers.

"I've waited all my life for this." His warm, fragrant breath wafted the words into her ear. His lips were kissing her ear, nibbling at it, his tongue licking the sensitive skin around the lobe. "I've wanted it forever. . . ."

"So have I," she breathed in return. The words left her before she even knew she was going to speak, and as they floated in the air she shivered with the truth of them. This was the antithesis of the aloneness that had been a fact of her existence for as long as she could remember; this was the fulfillment she had yearned for without even knowing the depth of her need. In that moment she knew beyond any doubt that she'd been looking for him all her life.

He hovered above her, his heavy-lidded eyes drinking in her body and her soul. His long legs moved between hers, and the ecstasy of his skin making contact with hers filled her senses.

Then he came into her, and when he did he took her mouth again with a fierceness of wanting that drew on the very essence of her being. Their coming together was a sensation to glory in; the ecstasy of it and the erotic hunger it created made her tremble with their power. This was right, this was perfect, this was a whole new dimension that she had never known existed.

He tore his lips from hers and pressed them against her ear, her neck, her face, and then to her mouth again as the passion that had been dormant in them both for too long began growing and growing, carrying them in a wild, uncontrollable spiral higher and then even higher.

She drew him into her with all her strength, with all the joy of loneliness released, and they spun together on that rhythm of primitive passion up and up to the very peak of sweet torture until the world fell away beneath them as if they had whirled off the edge of a precipice.

Afterward they just held each other, damp and trembling, savoring the closeness, the sated intimacy of their shaken bodies. His head rested quietly against hers; she could taste the sweat on his cheek.

Then she felt him tense. "Tracey?"

"Yes?"

"I told you the truth. I've waited all my life for this."
The words lay between them, unfinished. "But it's
come too late."

She sat up, searching his eyes. "Davis . . ."

He placed a finger across her lips to silence her.

"I came over here tonight to talk to you, Tracey . . .
to explain why I left you so abruptly before," he said,
his voice very low.

The words seemed to compound the uneasiness in
him, and restlessly he moved around and over her to
stand up, his long frame tense in the dimness of the
room.

He reached for his shirt and pulled it on. "I didn't
intend for this to happen . . . ever," he said harshly.

"Davis, it's all right. . . ."

"No." He slipped into his slacks and began to button
the shirt. "Don't talk, just listen."

Chilled, suddenly aware that she was naked, she
reached for her dress and wrapped it around her like a
shawl.

"You're somebody special, Tracey. You touch me in
a way that nobody else ever has. But I need to leave
you alone. I have to. This is no good for either of us."

Stunned, she stared at him. "I thought it seemed
pretty good for both of us," she told him, trying to keep
her bruised lips from trembling. "But I guess I must
have been mistaken."

He came back to her and sat beside her. In the
dimness his eyes were dark, his face tortured. He
pulled her hair up on one side and wound his fingers

into it, holding it so he could see her face and keep her head still at the same time.

"That isn't what I meant, love," he said softly, his voice vibrant with single-minded determination, willing her to understand. "This was wonderful. It's a night that I'll never forget." He rocked her head gently in his hand as he kept her eyes on his.

"But it's no good for us because we both know we can't stop with just this. This can't be something brief and casual, stuck off in some remote corner of our lives."

She stared at him wordlessly.

He went on. "And I don't see how it can be what it should be."

She was trembling with the finality in his voice, shaking with the effort to get her bearings. His eyes were boring into her, trying to force her to accept what he said.

"I've only loved one other woman," he said, his tone painfully gentle. "And I failed her." He watched her for another long minute, and when he spoke again his voice was raw with the anguish that tormented him. "Tracey, I couldn't live with it if I failed you."

He took his hand away and stood up, moving rapidly to the dim rectangle of the door. He turned back as if he wanted to speak again, but the aching silence held them both captive.

With one last look that begged her to understand he was gone.

Chapter Seven

That look and those words haunted her for the rest of the weekend. She lay awake during the nights; she didn't sleep at all until Saturday, when she napped fitfully for a while in the late, hot afternoon. She rode Foxfire for a long time and began to work with Trampas, but the animals and the sunshine didn't perform their usual magic.

She was restless; she wanted to get away, but somehow she couldn't bring herself to leave. It was as if some primitive instinct was telling her to wait, because this was the place where she'd last seen Davis. There was no place she wanted to go except to find him, nothing she wanted to do except make him talk to her.

She could see no way that she could survive in this misery for even a day, but Monday morning finally came and she welcomed it with open arms. She would immerse herself in her work, in the animals that had always been her refuge, and she would get him out of her head at last.

He was haunting her so because she'd been terribly lonely for a long time, she thought, lonelier than she'd realized. But she'd lived with that ever since Eric had left, and before that for years and years; she could live with it again. For a blissful few minutes she'd fooled herself into thinking that it was over, that she had found someone, but she'd been wrong. All she had to do was admit that and get everything back into perspective.

She dressed for work, forcing her mind back to Southwest. She certainly had enough to do; for one thing she was no closer to buying more rhinos to join Maqu than she had been the day he'd arrived.

She went into work early, and after making the first of the day's endless pots of coffee she settled down at her desk to force her exhausted mind onto her least favorite task: writing a speech.

She was scheduled to give three more speeches in as many weeks, one to the Chamber of Commerce in Tucson, one to a women's club in Scottsdale and one to a service club in Phoenix. There would probably be people in the service club who'd heard her speech the previous week to Phoenix's Chamber of Commerce, so she wanted to find a different way to bring them the same message, that Southwest—especially the preserve —needed their support.

She had just found a clean legal pad and was

searching for a pen when the phone on her desk shrilled. She stared at it. It was far too early for regular business.

Finally she reached for the receiver. "Southwest. Tracey Johnston."

"Tracey," Davis answered. "This is Davis. How are you this morning?"

Her fingers froze around the telephone at the same instant that white-hot resentment leaped in the pit of her stomach. He sounded as if he'd never met her outside the office, as if they were business acquaintances and nothing more. *How do you THINK I am?* she screamed silently. *Just how do you think I could possibly be this morning?*

She waited a second or two while she fought for control of her voice. "Fine, thanks," she managed at last. "And you?"

He hesitated almost imperceptibly before he said in that same impersonal tone, "Fine. I'm wondering whether you could drop by my house tomorrow night around seven. We need to get started on the plans for the snow leopard enclosure."

How could he expect her to come to his house? She'd been desperate for him to talk to her, but if this was all he had to say, she didn't ever want to see him again, much less spend an evening in his home!

"I don't think so, Davis," she answered coolly. Her mind whirled; she was dizzy with the onslaught of questions and feelings. How could she have spent the weekend desperate to see him again, *longing* for an explanation from him about his leaving her like that, when obviously he'd spent his time thinking not about her, but about Diane Grant's precious snow leopards?

"If you have something else planned, you really need to cancel it," he insisted. "The board is coming here for an afternoon meeting, and I want to get our preliminary planning under way immediately, just as soon as they've made official acceptance of the donation."

She didn't answer.

"You're welcome to come to the meeting itself, of course, if you'd like," he went on smoothly. "I know you don't really enjoy them, though, and you won't need to be here to represent Gerald; he's coming as his first step toward returning to work. I don't know whether you've talked with him, but he has his doctor's approval to attend a few isolated meetings and then to come back to the office half-days for a while."

So he'd been talking to Gerald that weekend, too, in addition to pondering the snow leopards. How energetic of him.

"I haven't talked with him yet," she said. "But he'll probably call me later today."

"Probably," he agreed briskly. "Well, how about it, Tracey? Can I expect you?"

"Look, Davis," she said, trying to match the efficient tone of his voice, "if Gerald is going to be there, why not just have him stay on and discuss the project with you? It sounds as if he'll be able to work with you on it after all."

"No," he said flatly. "We both agree that it should

still be you and I. I'll see you at seven tomorrow evening."

He hung up before she could say anything else, and she sat, holding the buzzing receiver to her ear. Her eyes narrowed, and she gave the ceramic giraffe in the corner the look she'd have loved to give Davis. "High-handed, arrogant tyrant!" she muttered.

The ranchhouse was located several miles into the property from the spot where they'd recaptured Maqu, and as she drove toward it Tracey tried to prepare herself to see him. If they were going to be forced together until this project was completed, she had to get her emotions under control. She'd never be able to function if she kept swinging back and forth between desperately wishing for the touch of his body on hers and cold fury at his seeming nonchalance about the whole thing.

If only he hadn't been so cryptic when he'd left her Friday night, if only he'd explained what he was talking about! Most of all, if only he had had *something* personal to say when he'd called her that morning!

Tears blurred her eyes as she pulled into the sweeping circle drive in front of his house and sat for a minute trying to sort out the thoughts pounding in her head, the protests to fate that she was holding inside when she really wanted to shout them to the heavens.

They'd been close, so close for a little while. They'd made love! He'd told her that he'd been waiting his whole life for her! She'd truly shared her body and her spirit with someone for the first time, and she'd thought that he was doing the same.

But the whole experience had been nothing to him. He wasn't going to explain anything to her; he'd probably never even refer to it again. He was acting as if he'd already forgotten all about it.

She took the keys from the ignition and dropped them into her bag, straightening her shoulders before she got out of the car. Well, she'd forget about it, too, in time, she thought. And tonight she was going to act as if she already had.

She drew a long breath and looked around her as she approached the top of the long flight of steps leading down to the front entry. She'd concentrate on the house, she decided, not only to fulfill the promise she'd made to tell Lottie "absolutely everything" about the design and furnishings, but to keep her mind off the man who owned the place.

Lottie had eagerly told her everything she'd heard about Davis's house, from the fact that an architect had come all the way from San Francisco to design it to the rumor that it was famous for fifty-mile views from some of the windows. Now as Tracey looked at the way it was situated on the edge of a deep gorge called Pima Canyon she decided that the rumor was probably true.

Her eyes followed the sprawling lines of the red-tiled roof. The house was white stucco and surrounded by its elaborate landscaping, and there seemed to be a porch on every side, all of them decorated with Spanish arches.

She began to descend the steps, trying not to think

about Davis at all as she reached the portico at the center of the main portion of the house. Then she could think about nothing else because he was standing there, opening the door before she even rang.

Her breath caught as her eyes took him in, casual and relaxed in perfectly cut tan western-styled slacks and a white silk shirt, its open collar startling against his tanned skin. Would she ever be able to see him without this terrible unsteady feeling overtaking her?

The rapid flicker of pleasure in his clear blue gaze said clearly that he'd been waiting for her, that he was glad to see her, but his tone when he spoke put a distance between them. "Tracey, come in," he invited, the perfect, genial host. "I'm glad you could make it."

He led her across the broad tile-floored entry hall and down a corridor into a room that seemed to be all glass and weathered dark wooden beams. "I've brought our work in here so we can watch night fall across the Santa Ritas," he said, gesturing toward the purple mountains in the distance. "And Marquita has promised to bring us some Margaritas and some snacks or some coffee, whatever you prefer."

"Coffee will be fine," she said, sinking into the deeply cushioned L-shaped couch that he took her to. She certainly didn't need an alcoholic drink; she was having enough trouble keeping all her faculties intact being this close to him.

He stepped to the door to ask his housekeeper to bring the coffee, then sat across a low square table from Tracey. Briskly he began taking papers from some folders that he had stacked there.

She sat up straighter and pulled a small pad and a pen from her bag. There was nothing to bring them together but business, she reminded herself. He was remembering that, and she certainly could, too.

"How did the board meeting go?" she asked.

"We accomplished a lot, I think." He was looking at the papers in front of him, and not at her.

"How was Gerald?"

He glanced up at her then, and his eyes were very blue. But they told her nothing. They said nothing about the evening they'd spent on *her* sofa making love.

His voice was low and pleasant, but it was as noncommital as his eyes. "He seemed fine, but he said he tires very easily."

"That's what he told me on the phone this afternoon," she answered, drawing aimlessly on the small rectangle of yellow paper propped on her knee. "But he's determined to come back to work soon. I'm going to meet with him the day after tomorrow and try to bring him up to date on everything; then he'll start coming to the office for the occasional half-day." She frowned and bit at the end of her pen. "I'm looking forward to some help, but I just have a feeling that he's rushing his recovery."

"Well, whether he is or not, he certainly won't be able to take over all his duties at once, and you'll still have too much to do." He smiled, and her pulse slowed for a second, then began beating again, almost imperceptibly faster. "That's why I asked the board this afternoon to give you a helper."

"A helper? Who? What do you mean?" she asked as

Marquita came into the room with a large tray of coffee and dainty desserts.

"Peggy. We're going to have her take over some of the speaking engagements and public relations functions that have been taking up your time. She'll be sort of a goodwill ambassador for Southwest. Bud Mattson's going to arrange for her to do some shopping mall openings, a couple of television talk shows, some club meetings like you've been doing. You know the kind of thing." He paused to pour a cup of coffee for her and then one for himself. "Good publicity will generate interest that can bring in thousands more visitors each year, not to mention increased contributions," he went on. "We're going to make it a permanent position and replace Peggy when she goes back to school in the fall."

She stared at him, aghast, her mind scrambling to absorb everything he'd said. "But, Davis, this is absurd! One day Peggy is going to bring down the wrath of her college and the media on our heads, and the next she's going to be running around all over the country telling everyone how great we are! I don't understand this. What happened?"

"You moved Cody out of her territory and that pacified her."

"*Or* you moved Peggy to a more glamorous job and *that* did the trick," she replied coldly.

"No, she'd already dropped all her threats. She did that as soon as she found out she wouldn't be working with Cody anymore."

She stared at him angrily, wondering what to believe,

trying to see beneath the surface of this startling news. Then she remembered the way he'd started breaking the news to her just now. He'd obviously been trying to butter her up so she'd agree that they really did need to spend the extra money that this salary would require.

He hadn't given Peggy this job to keep Tracey from having too much to do; he'd done it for Peggy! Just what *was* the girl to him, after all? She must be something more than just an old family friend if he'd gone to the extreme of creating a whole new job for her.

That idea spread through her and turned her cold, even as she felt her cheeks flush with warmth. There was no way she would ever understand him, she thought. Friday night she'd felt that she could sense his thoughts and feelings as if they were her own; she'd never have believed that she wasn't the only woman he wanted. But then he'd left her with that terrible finality of "It's no good for us." And now this.

He was still talking, and she dragged her attention away from her thoughts. "We decided that the best way to utilize this publicity is to use every cent we can get our hands on to buy one of several species that aren't seen in too many zoos, maybe a Matschie's tree kangaroo, a pair of white-cheeked gibbons, or a Bali mynah. Then Peggy's P.R. campaign can spread the news of our new additions."

He paused to take a cookie, waiting for her reaction.

When she spoke her voice was high, brittle. "Southwest can't afford that, Davis," she said. "Those animals won't be cheap. And there's the extra salary on top of that. I don't know what you're planning to pay Peggy, but when you replace her in the fall you'll have to come up with a good amount to attract and hold a competent person. All that will do is siphon away more money from the preserve."

"But ultimately it's for the *good* of the preserve," he said firmly, his eyes holding hers. "This will be a small investment compared to the benefits it can bring in."

She fought to keep the turmoil of her emotions from her face. It was an accomplished fact, she knew. He'd already had his obedient little board of directors rubber stamp the whole thing; they would have agreed with him that this was a necessary way to spend the money they'd told her they didn't have. And she could tell from the tone of his voice that there was no hope of changing anything they had done.

He sipped his coffee. "You'd probably be the logical one to set up appearances for Peggy and help her plan her presentation," he said. "She can take the ones that are already on your calendar, and the two of you can follow up any leads that you have for others. Just work them all around the ones Bud is going to find for her."

"All right," she said, speaking with careful precision. "I'll help Peggy work up a presentation, and I'll set up a schedule for her, but then, Davis, I'm going to take every minute that her job saves from my schedule to work for support for the preserve. There's no way that I'm going to sit around for *three years* and do absolutely nothing when I might be able to save even one species from extinction!"

She was furious that she had had to accept this

assignment without having had one word to say about
its conception, and tears of anger trembled just behind
her lids. But she met his gaze steadily, just as she had
the whole time she was speaking, and as he stared back
at her she saw his carefully impersonal expression
change. There was something there that reminded her
of the way he'd looked at her in the candle glow that
night in her house, a look that made her remember his
hands loosening her hair from its braid.

His eyes swept over her, drinking in every inch of her
pale yellow silk tunic and the matching pants she wore.

If she had subconsciously chosen the outfit with its
high draped neck and long sleeves for concealment, the
effort had failed. She must have wanted it to keep his
eyes from igniting her bare skin and making it long for
his hands as well, she thought now, but she felt them in
spite of it. And she could taste his blistering lips against
her own.

How could she be such a fool? she berated herself
mentally. One second ago she had hated him passionately, and now she was remembering his kisses with
equal passion. She ought to get up and walk out this
instant.

Instead she tore her eyes away from him. She played
with the rolled hem of her tunic and stared at it, then at
the patterns in the Navajo rug at her feet.

"Tracey," he said, and the one word was a caress in
itself. "Walk out into the courtyard with me. Let's relax
and talk for a minute before we try to work."

That pulled her eyes back to his, and the soft gleam
in their blue depths drew her to her feet. She rose and

followed him across the room, then walked beside him down a long hallway with a floor of fired Mexican tile.

"I told your friend, Cody, to come by and ride sometime if he likes. He loves horses, but he doesn't own one."

"He can't afford one, I'm sure. That's really nice of you, Davis. I know he'll enjoy your horses."

He brushed away the compliment. "I hope so." He opened a set of wide French doors and held them for her.

She stepped out into an enclosed courtyard that was surrounded on three sides by the house. It was as luxurious as the rest of his home, and it immediately drew her into its spell. It seemed a separate world made just for them, a world just of the senses; the scents of oleanders and jasmine floated out to surround them, and the waterfall in the corner tumbled over the rocks and down into the canyon below in a rhythm that matched their heartbeats.

He led her to a bench under a large palm tree growing in the center of the lush landscape. His thigh touched hers, and unreasoning desire leaped in her.

She fastened her eyes on the night sky above the waterfall, trembling a little. Then, she caught the spicy scent of his aftershave, the warm smell of him, and she wanted nothing but to turn into his arms, to drive her fingers into his hair and bring his lips to hers.

But no, she thought. He'd probably make love to her and then calmly announce that he had business elsewhere. No matter what he said, he was sure to leave her before she could even catch her breath. She wasn't going through that again. This meeting was business, and she was going to keep it that way.

"We haven't even mentioned the snow leopards yet," she remarked, relieved to find that her voice was normal when she spoke. It seemed impossible, with her blood pounding at such a rate.

"Before we even begin to talk about that project, Tracey, we need to discuss something else," he said quietly. "I think if we can get a bit closer together philosophically, that project will move a whole lot faster when we do get into it."

She turned to him with a rueful look. "I seem to recall a couple of occasions when you assured me that we already agree philosophically," she said. "You've been telling me all along that our goals are the same, that you want the preserve as much as I do."

He laughed, and the low, rich sound threatened to completely destroy her concentration. "I know," he said.

He looked down into her face for a long moment, and when he spoke again it was with such caring in his voice that tears, a different kind this time, threatened her again. "Tracey," he said softly, "I know what your dream is. I know how much you want it."

His hand brushed her cheek, and then one finger traced the shape of her face. His eyes never left hers. "I wish I could just magically give you everything you want right this minute," he said softly.

He gave her a smile that made her begin to melt. "We really are going to do all the things you have your heart set on," he went on. "It won't be long until you'll be breeding rare animals and saving whole species the way you want. Just don't be impatient. Let us get this whole thing on a sound financial basis."

The tone was lulling, but the words were familiar, and the old tired frustration shot through her. She pulled away and looked at him very straight. "Davis," she said, and her voice trembled, "listen to me. We can't *wait* three years for the preserve. If we do, by then we'll be firmly set on the wrong track and we'll never recover. We'll be nothing but a tourist attraction full of exotic oddities."

"It may not be three years," he answered. "When our goodwill ambassador—"

"I don't want to hear any more about that goodwill ambassador business!" she burst out. "I'll train Peggy, and I'll do what I have to do, but that whole plan is nothing but another step away from what I'm working for!"

"If you'd *think* about it for five minutes, you'd want to hear about it," he retorted sarcastically. "This idea can raise a whole lot of that money you've been agitating for. It's the quickest way *to* your goals, Tracey, not away from them."

She continued to stare at him, her anger building by the minute.

"Give me some time, Tracey. Give me time and I'll get you what you want."

"Time!" she scoffed, jumping to her feet. "If that's all you can say, I'm going. I'm sick of hearing that excuse."

He stood, too, moving swiftly to block her way. "You

may have heard the word before, but it's never reached your brain. If you'd ever think about it, you'd know I'm telling you the truth."

Furious now, she tried to step around him. "I'm leaving, Davis. This discussion is becoming completely insane."

"Insane or not, it isn't finished." He caught her arm. She tried to pull away, but his grip was too strong to break, and she succeeded only in being pulled closer to him. Anger blinded her; she could hardly see his face.

She opened her mouth to demand that he let her go, but before she could speak his mouth came down on hers. She tried to get her hands up and onto his chest so she could push him away, but his arms tightened around her, and his lips burned into hers, branding them. His teeth and his tongue crushed against hers as if saying that he would make her change her mind.

Then, without warning, the message changed. His tongue became a seducer, stroking hers, caressing it, luring her to respond. Its wild sweetness shot through to the soul of her; it made the warm sensations of their lovemaking come flooding back to wash through her in an irresistible tide.

Her lips fell open to him, and she put her hands into his hair, taking him eagerly with the hunger that had pulsed in her for all those endless days just past. The courtyard became their private universe again, a place where no one else existed. She breathed in the fragrances of the flowers and let the tumbling of the waterfall beat in her ears.

His hands roamed her back, her shoulders, her rib

cage; they moved to the swell of her breasts, causing their swollen tips to yearn toward his touch. His hands were magic, and their warm provocation went through her clothing to find her skin as if the flimsy fabric wasn't even there.

When the kiss ended at last she was still melded against the length of him, and his hands were still stroking her, exciting and at the same time gentling her. She tilted her head to fit her cheek into the cup of his hand, and he kissed her ear.

Then he whispered into it, "Tracey, all this resistance of yours is only going to slow things down more for Southwest. Work with me, trust me. I'm trying . . ."

His words jolted her back to reality. *That* was the reason he was making love to her! He didn't care about her; he was only trying to shut her up, to stop her constant resistance to having money go to his precious display zoo instead of to the preserve!

It explained everything. That was what he'd been trying to tell her that night at her house: There was no way they could have anything lasting in their personal lives because they were so incompatible professionally. He had no hopes of changing her views permanently, but he thought that he could temporarily gain her cooperation with kisses and caresses.

Hurt and betrayal sliced into her like twin swords, and she went cold all the way through. This little excursion into the sensuous courtyard "to relax," "to get closer together philosophically," was nothing but a cruel charade, an attempt to manipulate her so she wouldn't make too much fuss about the money for new zoo animals and the new job he'd given his darling Peggy.

She twisted in his arms and tore herself away, desperate to escape. She was as furious with herself for succumbing to this spurious enchantment as she was with him for creating it.

"Don't do this to me, Davis!" she cried. "Don't kiss me!" She took a step backward, frantic to put some distance between them. "Don't touch me!"

A sob caught in her throat, and she felt the sting of tears at last. "Don't even talk to me. Davis, leave me alone!"

Chapter Eight

Tracey glanced at her watch as she and Gerald came out of the Italian Garden Restaurant. She wanted to suggest that they go observe Peggy as she made a presentation at a new shopping mall nearby, but she was afraid that it would make Gerald too tired. They had had to postpone this dinner meeting for over a week while he recovered from the board meeting and one half-day at the office.

"Let's drive over to El Camino Mall and see how Peggy's doing," he suggested as they reached his car.

"All right. I was just wishing we could do that, but I thought maybe you should go home to rest."

"Oh, I think I'm up to a couple more hours out on the town," he joked as he got in behind the wheel. "I'm feeling lots better today; this hasn't been nearly as stressful as that board meeting at Davis's house."

Davis. She looked out her window as they drove, but she saw nothing of the streets of Tucson. All she could see was Davis, his face sculpted into unmoving stone as she told him furiously to leave her alone.

Well, he had taken her at her word. It had been over a week, and she hadn't seen or heard from him. And that was what she wanted.

She had half-expected him to call, though, simply because he'd been so insistent that the two of them had to make the plans for the snow leopards, and that they had to do it immediately. Well, evidently he was going ahead without her, and she didn't care. He and Gerald, or he and Bud Mattson, or he and *Peggy* could do it. All she wanted was never to see him again so she wouldn't have to be reminded of how he'd tried to deceive her.

"You okay?" Gerald asked. "You're awfully quiet."

His question brought her back to the present, and she was surprised to see that they were already back on Highway 86. She pushed the thoughts of Davis away.

"I'm fine," she answered, smiling at him. "Just thinking." She searched for something to say before he could offer a penny for her thoughts.

They were approaching the sprawling new shopping center, so she said, "We probably should go in the main entrance. We set up the exhibits in the middle of the central atrium."

They parked, then walked across the crowded parking lot and into the mall, chatting about the public appearances that had been planned for Peggy so far and about the new publicity campaign in general.

"There's our display," she said as they reached the center corridor. "Looks like we have quite a crowd."

A smiling Peggy was standing under a large banner that proclaimed "National Zoo and Aquarium Month." She was running a projector, flashing slides of Southwest's animals onto a screen that had been set up under the banner and keeping up a running commentary at the same time. Tracey and the education curator's staff had prepared all her material and she had memorized it, but her delivery was so relaxed and natural that it seemed spontaneous.

A sizable crowd was watching the slides and listening to Peggy, and several other people were wandering around, some reading the information displayed in the static exhibits, others watching the fish in the two large aquariums that had been brought in to flank Peggy's booth.

They listened to Peggy as she finished her prepared comments and then began to field questions from the audience. "She does a good job, doesn't she?" Tracey asked, glancing up to get Gerald's reaction.

"Yes," he answered. He smiled at Tracey. "Probably because she's had such a good teacher."

"I can't take the credit," she demurred. "I have to admit that she's studied like crazy and done everything I told her to."

"I had my doubts when Davis said he wanted her for the job; I thought he just wanted to do something for his favorite little girl," Gerald said thoughtfully, looking back at Peggy. "But I should've known he's too good a businessman for that. Peggy's poised, and her looks and personality draw a lot of attention."

"Yes," Tracey agreed. "When I went to observe her first speech, the one she made to the Western Women's Club, I was impressed. Much as I hate for all that money to go into a public relations campaign, I have to admit that it might do some good."

She followed his gaze as he looked the exhibit over carefully. "Gerald, I've thought of something that would attract even more of a crowd in a situation like this," she said. "Live animals. If Peggy could bring one or two of the more cuddly, interesting ones, she'd really be dynamite."

He began to nod enthusiastically as she talked. "Good idea, Tracey. In fact, great idea!"

Thoughtfully she fastened her eyes on the girl. "I talked to Peggy about it today, but she really shies away from the concept."

"Then she might not be good at it."

"Well . . . I don't know. I'm not going to give up."

"Has she had any experience with animals at all?"

"Hardly any. She's ridden horses a little bit on her grandfather's ranch, but she's never really taken to them."

"Well, you might ask her over to your house and let her watch you with your horses," he suggested. "And if you want, even take one or two of the zoo animals over there, too. Let her observe you handling some animals in an atmosphere that's more relaxed. Let her get some hands-on experience with you directing her."

She nodded, thinking it over. "That might help. I think one of the reasons she's had trouble when I've tried to help her handle animals at Southwest has been the fact that she's a little intimidated by the experienced keepers."

"Then this might be the answer. Let's try it."

"I will. In fact, I'm going to start thinking about which animal to use first."

"Oh, no! I don't want you concentrating on *that* this evening," he complained, laughing. "You've been working far too hard since I've been sick, and even dinner tonight was business. Let's just relax and wander around the stores for a while, and then we'll come back by here about the time for the keepers to come for the fish." He chuckled, took her arm and started walking away as he finished. "If we stand around here too long, we'll end up answering questions for some of these people."

They wandered through the mall, idly looking into shop windows, but nothing attracted them, and finally they bought some sodas and settled onto a bench across from a sporting goods store.

"I suppose I should go in there and get myself outfitted," he said with a grin. "If I'm going up to Lake Mead with Davis Turnbo, I'd better be ready."

Davis's name slashed into her for the second time that evening. "What do you mean? I haven't heard anything about a trip to Lake Mead."

"Oh, you remember. It's that convention of legislators and businessmen from all over the Southwest.

They're meeting to talk about tourism and conservation and who knows what else."

"Oh, yes. But I thought they were going to meet in Denver."

"At first they were, but now it's been changed," he explained. "And the organizing committee has asked Southwest to send someone to talk about our needs and our potential."

"Oh, Gerald, that's wonderful!" she said enthusiastically. "It's a chance to go right to the major source of our financial support! Talk to everyone you see about money to get the preserve started. Don't forget to mention white rhinos."

"I won't. I'll spend the whole time lobbying." He grinned at her. "Very tactfully, of course."

She nodded, smiling back at him wryly. "So that's why you're going instead of sending me," she said drolly. "You think I'd be my usual undiplomatic self."

"I didn't say that, *you* did," he replied, laughing. "It's my job to go because most of the talk will be about finances and not animals. *I'm* the business administrator and you're the zoologist, remember?"

"I know," she said with a smile. "I'm just teasing you."

He took a sip of his drink. "Anyway, Davis is going, too, as one of the business leaders and as board chairman for Southwest, so he and I are going to fly up there in his Lear jet."

She bent her head and let her hair fall across her face, her fingers restlessly twisting the straw in her cup.

It was certainly fortunate that Gerald was getting well so he'd be able to go. It would have been an absolutely impossible situation if *she'd* been the representative chosen from Southwest. She couldn't go to Lake Mead or anyplace else with Davis Turnbo.

Tracey turned sideways and held the door open with her hip as she balanced a tray of snacks with both hands. She smiled a little as she glanced at Peggy, who was slumped on the chaise lounge at the edge of the patio. It was the first time she'd ever seen Peggy rumpled, she thought. Poor girl, she was not only disheveled, she was exhausted.

"I think we deserve something to drink and a bit of relaxation after a long hard day at Southwest and a session with the hard-headed Trampas," Tracey said. "Don't you?"

Peggy nodded wearily. Her usually confident smile was a little askew. "This is really hard work, Tracey. And it makes me so nervous. I don't think I'll ever get the hang of it."

"Oh, yes, you will," Tracey answered with a teasing smile as she set the tray on the table between them. "You started with a horse today, and by next week you'll probably be training elephants. Maybe you can take an elephant with you to your speech in Phoenix."

"Please, Tracey!" Peggy said, laughing. "Let's not rush things. I've just said I'll try. I'm not guaranteeing anything."

Tracey handed her a cold glass of soda. "Trying is all

I ask. Really, Peggy, I think you put your finger on your biggest problem when you said you get so nervous. An animal can sense that. . . ."

She was interrupted by the sound of hooves in her driveway. Then she heard them moving off the gravel and onto the grass of her front yard.

A moment later Cody's voice called, "Tracey, are you home?"

She and Peggy exchanged a surprised look. "Back here, Cody," she called back. "On the patio." Before she could go to show him the way around the house he appeared.

"Cody! It's good to see you," she said warmly. Then she glanced at Peggy. "Have you two met? . . ."

"Yes," he said, enveloping Peggy in his flashing smile. "I saw you in the staff meeting a couple of times," he said to her. "I could never forget your face, but I'm sorry, I don't remember your name. I'm Cody Howard."

Peggy stared at him. "Hi," she said weakly. "I'm Peggy Smalley."

"This is a surprise," Tracey told him. "I couldn't imagine who was showing up at my house on horseback."

"I was over at Mr. Turnbo's, riding, and I just got the idea to come see you," he said. "Remember when you told me where you live?"

She tried to pretend that she hadn't heard Davis's name. "Yes," she said, smiling at him. "You're very good at following directions."

He grinned. "You're always so busy at work that I never see you, so I decided to come to your house."

"Cody, sit here and I'll run in and get you a cold drink," she said, indicating the chair beside hers. "I'll be back in just a minute."

He sat down, taking off his dusty hat and laying it on the ground beside his chair. "Aren't you a friend of Davis's?" he was asking Peggy as Tracey left them. "I thought I saw you with him one time at Southwest."

His manner as he spoke to Peggy was full of his usual easy charm, and suddenly Tracey realized that he didn't know how Peggy felt about him. He had no idea that she'd refused to associate with him, or that her complaints had been the reason he was no longer on the guide staff.

By the time she came back with Cody's drink he and Peggy were chatting easily, talking mostly about Davis, it seemed.

"But wasn't it an awfully long ride from Davis's ranch to here?" Peggy asked.

"Not as far as you'd think. I came cross country," he answered.

"But weren't you coming across other people's land?" Peggy asked. Her wide green eyes were absorbing every detail of him as he slouched gracefully in his chair.

"It wasn't fenced," he told her. "And anyhow, I never pay much attention to boundaries." He had a rakish glint in his brown eyes. "You've heard about rules being made to be broken?" he went on with a spoofing bravado. "Well, boundaries are made to be crossed."

"Oh, you can't mean that," Peggy said, giggling. She ran one hand over her hair to smooth it, and as she looked into Cody's eyes all the old sparkle was back in her smile.

"Cody, how's Sand?" Tracey asked. "I haven't had time to come see him lately."

"Doing super," he said, taking a swig of soda. "He's eating like a champ, and he's getting to know I'm his keeper."

"Cody's hand raising a baby cougar," Tracey explained to Peggy. "That's his new assignment at Southwest."

"Oh," Peggy said. She turned back to Cody. "I'm trying to get used to being around animals more so I can handle some when I go out to publicize Southwest." She batted her lashes at him. "But it's really hard because they make me so nervous."

"Then they know that," he told her. "You've just gotta decide that you're the boss and then the animal will know it, too."

"Is that the secret?" she asked, looking at Cody as if those were the wisest words she'd ever heard, as if Tracey hadn't told her the very same thing a half hour before.

Tracey looked intently from one of them to the other. They were smiling at each other with the flirtatious confidence of two people who were finding each other very attractive—and with the obliviousness of two people who didn't even remember that a third person was there.

She sipped her drink and watched them, trying to sort things out. What in the world was Peggy doing? Was she just responding for a moment to Cody's natural charm and good looks? If so, why, after her initial reaction to him?

Of course Peggy had a very practical outlook, Tracey thought as she listened to their banter. Maybe since Cody had been around this long without making any trouble, she had decided that he was harmless.

But what would she want with Cody if Davis were interested in her?

Tracey took a long drink of her own soda and then sat, nervously tapping her nail against her glass. No doubt Peggy had her reasons, she thought. She probably wanted Cody to do something for her, just as Davis had had an ulterior motive for making love to Tracey.

You'd better watch out, Cody, she thought, watching Peggy touch him lightly on the arm as she laughed at something he'd said. You'd better watch out. You may be street smart, but you're no more a match for Peggy than I am for Davis. Dreamers like us never see reality until it's too late.

Tracey finished reading the last page of the speech Peggy had asked her to edit and, stretching wearily, glanced at her watch. Five-thirty. No wonder she was tired.

She stacked the papers together in order and slipped

a paper clip onto them. Lottie had probably gone home by now, but she'd put them on the secretary's desk so she could type the final draft first thing in the morning.

She went out into the reception area, but before she put the speech into Lottie's basket she stood for a minute, double checking a statistic, one knee resting on the secretary's chair.

"I really don't know whether to say hello or not. I keep remembering that you told me not to talk to you."

The rich tones of his voice were as familiar as the memory of his embrace, and they sent an intoxicating thrill trembling along every one of her nerves. All the blood in her body pounded into her head, and the printed words on the page swam in front of her eyes.

Finally she looked up. He was standing in the doorway, leaning casually against the frame. He was wearing faded jeans and a western shirt; he was again the dusty cowboy she'd first seen riding toward her across the sand.

Her hands shook a little as she put the papers onto the desk and she didn't answer him. She felt the color rise to her cheeks. Damn! How could he *still* do this to her? Well, this time she wouldn't let him.

She forced her eyes to meet his. "Did you want to see Gerald?"

He considered the question. "I came to see Gerald," he said finally, "but I wanted to see you." There was that intonation again, that verbal caress, as if the tips of his fingers were brushing a path down the side of her neck.

In a blinding epiphany she recognized his words as

the echo of a cry pulsing deep inside her. She had wanted to see him, too. She hadn't known how much until this very minute.

They didn't move or speak for what seemed an eon to her. The pain was in his eyes, the mysterious hurt she'd seen there the night they made love in her moonlit house. And . . . the desire was there, too. The desire that never failed to kindle an answering fire in her.

The sudden threat of tears stung her eyes as the unsettling warmth spread through her. She'd kept it away from her for so long. And she had to keep it, and him, away from her from now on, because she meant nothing to him.

She reached for her anger, hoping it would sustain her, but it was gone. Only hurt was in its place.

"Gerald didn't come in today," she told him, her voice the tiniest bit unsteady. "He called to say he isn't feeling well again."

He made a gesture of dismissal. "It's not important. I'll see him later."

He smiled, and the gesture caught at her heart. It was slow and sexy, and she wanted to hold his face in her hands. She wanted to taste his lips with her tongue. She wanted to feel the comfort of his skin on hers. She wanted to go to him and let him hold her and tell her that it was all a mistake, that he really did care about her after all. She wanted him to hold her forever.

She gathered all her strength. "Davis, go. Leave me."

"But, Tracey . . ."

"Davis, please," she begged. The tears materialized and stood on the ends of her lashes. "We have nothing to say to each other."

He hesitated, then drawled, "I disagree." He waited, but she was mute. Finally he said, in the assured tone that she'd come to know so well, "We'll talk, Tracey. Later, we'll talk." Then, without a good-bye, he was gone.

She listened to his footsteps die away in the empty hallway. As soon as they were gone she gathered up her things and left the office, trying not to think about him as she hurried out of the building into the shimmering heat of the late afternoon.

Chapter Nine

$\mathcal{T}$racey reached for the button on the desk phone without lifting her eyes from the letter in her hand.

"Yes, Lottie?" She read the last paragraph for the fourth time.

"Peggy Smalley's here. Do you have time to see her?"

"Yes, send her in."

In a moment Peggy's voice penetrated the fog that surrounded Tracey. "Well, I wish I'd get a letter if it'd make me that happy!"

Tracey transferred her smiling glance from the paper to Peggy. "This is something like getting a letter from Santa Claus without even writing to him first," she said. "Peggy, sit down and listen to this.

"'I am pleased to inform you that if Southwest can obtain the permissions necessary to import Dehli, I will contribute both her purchase price and the cost of having her shipped to Southwest.'" She looked up at Peggy, beaming.

Peggy beamed back as if all that happiness was contagious. "That's great news, all right," she said. "But maybe you should start at the beginning. What animal? Who's Dehli, and where's she coming from?"

"An Asian elephant. A *Ceylonese* elephant! Asian elephants are endangered, and the Ceylonese are the most endangered subspecies of all. There's an orphaned one in Sri Lanka, and a man in Phoenix who has business ties there heard about her. He's going to buy her for us!"

"Wonderful! But what's all that about permissions?"

"Oh, there's always tons of paperwork to getting an endangered animal shipped into the country—export permits, import permits, things like that." Tracey frowned. "We'll have to fill out all kinds of question-naires and forms. . . ."

"Don't tell me; I don't want to know," Peggy said, laughing. "It sounds like a long story, and I only have ten minutes until the fish and I have to leave for our next appearance."

Tracey laughed, too. "I'm sorry," she said. "Where are all of you going today?"

"To a library out in Canyon Verde. I'll get to show my filmstrip again." She sighed dramatically.

"Someday soon you'll have at least one of the animals on that filmstrip with you in the flesh," Tracey told her. "*That'll* keep every appearance from being just like the one before."

"True." Peggy thought about that possibility. "On second thought, maybe doing the same old filmstrip again really isn't all that bad."

Tracey chuckled. "Well, we'll keep working on that problem. You'd better tell me why you're here so you won't be late for the fish."

Peggy's pale complexion pinkened, and she hesitated for a minute, uncharacteristically at a loss for words. "I came by for . . . an apology, I suppose you'd call it," she said finally.

Tracey waited, her eyebrows raised in a question.

"I was wrong about Cody," Peggy said at last. "And I'm really embarrassed about being such a problem. I'm sorry, Tracey."

"I take it you're getting to know him better."

"Yes, and I think he's great. After we met at your house the other day I ran into him again over at Davis's. We rode together and had a lot of fun, and later Davis told me that he's gotten to know Cody and he really likes him." She blushed again and looked down at her long slender fingers. "We've seen each other several times and . . ."

"Peggy, you don't have to explain to me," Tracey told her. "Your position was understandable, considering the things we hear about convicts out on parole, and so on. It's just that Cody isn't really a convict, and I felt from the moment I met him that he was basically a good person."

"I agree with you now." The girl's eyes met Tracey's and the glow in them told Tracey that those words were a complete understatement. She looked so happy, so . . . why, she looked almost as if she were falling in love!

The idea made Tracey almost dizzy with amazement, but as she continued to watch and listen to the girl she knew that it was true. There was no way Peggy could have that look on her face and that tone in her voice when she talked about Cody if she was only trying to use him for some reason.

Immediately, against her will, her mind leapt to Davis and his apparent interest in Peggy. Peggy, obviously, was interested in no one but Cody.

But she wouldn't let herself think about it past that point. She forced her attention back to the girl and said, "Peggy, I'm just glad that you and Cody each have a new friend. Don't worry about the complaints you made. I'm willing to forget about them."

Peggy's wide green eyes were suddenly worried, imploring. "Tracey, does he . . . does Cody know? . . ."

"About your protests? No, I don't think so. I didn't tell him when I changed his assignment."

Peggy's shoulders slumped in relief under her uniform. "Good. I'll have to tell him sometime, because he might hear about it, but I don't want to yet." She stood up to go. "Tracey, thanks."

Tracey smiled at her. "You're welcome, Peggy. Say hello to Cody for me."

"I'm seeing him after work and I'll tell him," Peggy answered. "Bye."

"Bye."

After the girl had gone Tracey sat for a minute, shaking her head, thinking about the firm judgment

she'd made when Peggy had looked at Cody so flirta-
tiously that afternoon on her patio. She smiled ruefully
to herself. Well, that was one time when she'd been
totally wrong. And now she had the feeling that she
must have been wrong about the relationship between
Peggy and Davis, too.

Absently she picked up the small statue of a wilde-
beest from her desk and moved it around on the shiny
wood surface. If only she could have been that wrong
about Davis's motives concerning her! The thought
came suddenly, the sharp wish twisting hopelessly
inside her. If only everything really could be the way it
had seemed that night when they'd made love!

Despair washed over her, and she closed her eyes for
a second as if the gesture could blot it out, wanting to
hide from every feeling connected with him. She'd
driven herself like a madwoman these past few days to
keep from thinking about him.

Restlessly she pushed back her chair and went to the
wall of low bookshelves and cabinets where she kept all
her reference books. The letter about the proposed
donation of the Ceylonese elephant was the first really
good news she'd had in a long time, and she was going
to think about that instead of Davis. She intended to
make sure that it grew from a proposal into reality,
and that would take a lot of tedious work, dealing
with the often intimidating rules about the taking,
shipping and receiving of animals from an endangered
species.

She began to search for information about requirements for export permits from Sri Lanka, pulling out

several booklets that she thought might have them listed. She carried them and a copy of the regulations for import permits to her desk and sat down again, trying to force her thoughts to stay on the words on the page in front of her. She would immerse herself in technical information for the next hour or so and find out how to get the lengthy process of buying and shipping the elephant under way. Maybe she could have some of the preliminary research done when Gerald came in to work.

She worked for several minutes, gradually succeeding in escaping into the details of her work. She found some of the information she needed, then went back to the bookcase. She was crouching beside it, looking on the lowest shelf for more information, when the phone rang again.

With an exclamation of annoyance she stood up and reached for it. "Yes, Lottie?"

"It's Gerald, Tracey. He wants to talk to you."

Gerald's voice, when she took the call, was a shock. It sounded nothing like it had when she'd seen him the day before; it was almost as tired and weak as it had been when he was still in the hospital.

"Gerald! What's wrong?"

"I'm evidently having some sort of relapse," he said. "At least, that's what the doctor says. I've just come from his office."

"I can't believe it! Gerald, I'm so sorry."

"So am I," he said wryly. "The prospect of spending another week in bed certainly isn't very appealing."

"Is that what he told you to do?"

"Well, I may get by with just spending a couple of days resting, but we won't know until we try it. He says I've been doing too much too soon and I simply have to get more rest."

"Then get it. You don't want to end up back in the hospital."

"No, I don't. But I really hate to dump all this on you at the last minute."

"Don't worry about us; we can manage," she told him cheerfully. "We got used to it when you were in the hospital; we'll just save all the worst problems for when you come back," she teased. "Oh, and, Gerald, I need to tell you, we got the best news today. . . ."

"Tracey." His tone was one of amusement mixed with exasperation.

"Yes?"

"We don't have time to gossip now. You need to get a copy of my speech from Lottie and then go home and pack. We were planning to fly out at noon."

"What? Who? Fly where?"

"To Lake Mead. Eldorado Resort. I told you about it, Tracey. Tonight the legislators' convention begins."

She moved the receiver away from her ear, and for a minute she simply stared at it. He wasn't apologizing about dumping the regular chores and responsibilities of Southwest on her. He was asking her to go to Lake Mead and make a speech in his place.

He was sending her to Eldorado Resort with Davis Turnbo!

The idea made her feel almost dizzy, and she gripped the edge of the desk with one hand. He couldn't do this to her! She *couldn't* be alone with Davis. She couldn't handle that.

Finally she put the phone back to her ear, and when she could talk again, she interrupted. "Gerald, are you saying that now *I'm* to be Southwest's representative at that convention on tourism?"

"And conservation. Exactly. You'll deliver my speech tomorrow morning, and then you can just relax and talk to everyone you see about funding your breeding program for white rhinos. This is the chance you've been looking for, Tracey."

"But . . . I can't. Gerald, I simply cannot go up there in your place."

"Why not? You've made speeches before. Lots of them. Those legislators aren't any more intimidating than the other people you've spoken to."

"It . . . it isn't the speech that I can't do. I can handle that. It's . . . Gerald, I just can't."

"You most certainly can. You have to. Get the speech, go home and pack, and meet Davis Turnbo and his pilot at Mesa Field at noon."

When she arrived at the small public airfield that served the area around Southwest, Tracey parked in the fenced lot and took out her luggage, double checking to make sure that she had her briefcase, which held a copy of Gerald's speech.

She locked the car, then slipped the straps of her

suitcase over her shoulder and started across the pavement to the airport's one small building. She hoped that she'd brought everything she'd need; the whole time she'd been packing she'd hardly been able to think about anything but the fact that she'd be with Davis for the next three days.

As she reached the building she glanced briefly at her reflection in the glass door. At least the outfit she was wearing looked reasonably put together; the earth tones of her linen skirt and jacket blended with her eyes and hair, and the gold of her jewelry added a bright touch.

She shook her hair back from her face and opened the door. It was too late to worry about how she looked; now she had to worry about how to deal with the awkwardness of being alone with Davis for the flight to Lake Mead. That would be the worst of it; after they arrived she could surround herself with people and keep so busy that they wouldn't have time to talk.

She saw him as soon as she was inside, and suddenly her steps slowed. He was pacing back and forth in front of the glass wall that formed the west side of the terminal, looking out at the planes parked in the ramp area. He turned when he heard the door close, and when his eyes met hers she stopped where she was.

He came toward her, surprise, then pleasure, in his eyes.

"Tracey! I was expecting Gerald."

"He's ill again. Didn't he get in touch with you?"

"He may have tried, but I came straight here from a construction site. I've been a little hard to reach this morning." He reached to slide the handles of the suitcase off her shoulder just as she reached for them, and their fingers touched with a galvanic charge.

She looked away from him for a second, pretending to struggle with her second bag. She had to remember her resolution. This trip was going to be all business; there would be no intimate talk, despite what he had promised at her office.

"Gerald's doctor thinks he's been doing too much and that his hepatitis may recur if he doesn't rest," she explained, carefully keeping her voice impersonal. "I was the logical replacement."

"I'm glad," he said simply. "I'm sorry Gerald isn't feeling well, but I'm glad you're coming."

He slipped the suitcase onto his own shoulder and took the other bag from her. "My pilots are on board; we were just waiting for Gerald. I want to get to Eldorado in time to talk to Senator Crandall about some oil legislation before all the meetings start."

"Isn't he a member of the U.S. Senate?" she asked as he led her through the building and out onto the ramp area toward a shining beige and brown Lear jet.

"Yes. There will be several people from the federal government at the conference, as well as state government personnel from all over the Southwest."

She grimaced. "This gets worse and worse," she said as they reached the steps of the plane. "I have to make a speech."

He laughed. "They're only human. Don't worry about them."

"I am worried. I haven't even *read* the speech yet!"

"Don't worry, you'll do a good job," he said comfortingly.

They went up the steps into a luxurious cabin that seemed to be all oak trim and fawn-colored leather, and a man Davis introduced as his copilot came to put away the luggage.

Davis seated Tracey in one of the deep leather swivel chairs behind a round table, and when the copilot had gone forward to the cockpit he sat down across from her.

"Fasten your seatbelt," he said. "Then when we're airborne I'll get us something cold to drink."

"All right." She glanced at the bar built into the cabin to one side of the table. "You certainly have all the conveniences of home here, don't you?"

He shrugged and followed her glance to the heavy basket-weave drapes on the windows and the fine Indian prints on the walls. "I guess so," he said.

Their supply of small talk seemed suddenly exhausted. She busied herself with fastening her seatbelt, feeling tense and drained by the strain of keeping up this impersonal facade.

But she *wanted* everything on this trip to be impersonal, she thought, gritting her teeth as she forced the difficult buckle to work. It had to be. She had an important job to do, and she couldn't let him distract her.

She studied the delicately colored print on the wall to

one side of him, fighting to keep her eyes away from his face. She closed her eyes for a minute and tried to calm the onslaught of feeling. It was still so hard to admit that there had never been anything real between them, that all that closeness had existed only in her imagination. How could she have been so wrong? And how could she do her job when every time she looked up she saw his face?

She tried to think ahead to what she wanted to accomplish at Eldorado. Instead she remembered the look in his eyes when he'd stood in her office door that late afternoon, the look that had destroyed her anger and left this throbbing hurt in her. Well, that personal talk he'd mentioned then was an impossibility now. If just sitting near him and making polite conversation was this difficult, the emotional turmoil of discussing real feelings would destroy her ability to work entirely.

The noise of the engines starting floated in to them, and the plane began to move. She straightened and reached for her briefcase. She needed to concentrate all her time and energy on her speech and her lobbying. After all, her career was the only future she had.

As they became airborne he watched her as unobtrusively as he could, hating the guarded withdrawal that he sensed in her. Well, what could he expect? He never should have made love to her. He hadn't been fair to her. The pain of it pulled at him, as it had done for days.

But they could still be friends. She'd come into his life too late, and there was nothing he could do about that, but he could talk to her about it, he could tell her what the demons were that stood between them. He owed that to her and to himself.

In another moment he went to the bar and took two cans of soda from the refrigerator. She glanced up and then couldn't keep from watching his casual movements as he opened the ice bucket, put cubes into glasses and poured the drinks. The memory of those same sure hands sliding over her bare skin shimmered through her, and she raised her eyes to his face. Desire made her tremble.

She turned her head to stare out at the clouds they were flying over, her thoughts and feelings as fitful as their random white patterns.

He brought the filled glasses back to the table. "To your speech," he said, a teasing glint in his eyes. "May it be a success no matter how many people are there from Washington, D.C."

She managed to drag her thoughts back to her work and chuckle lightly at his joke. "My speech needs all the good thoughts it can get," she told him. "I'll probably have to rewrite it entirely. Gerald's ideas are very similar to mine, but our styles are certainly different."

"Well, if you get off whatever subject Gerald has planned, you can always talk about the latest romance at the zoo."

"What do you mean?"

"Cody and Peggy," he said, frowning worriedly. "What's going on with them?"

She raised one eyebrow, surprised that he'd made the same observation she had. She said noncommittally, "They seem to be making friends at last."

"I'm afraid it's more than that. Peggy came to see me yesterday and apologized to me for raising such a fuss about Cody. I got the distinct impression that she's more than a little infatuated with him."

She nodded. "She came by this morning and apologized to me, too. She said they're meeting after work today. Evidently they've found a lot in common."

"Or a lot that's different."

"The old ladies loving outlaws bit?"

He nodded. "It's just what we talked about before. Just what I was afraid of. The old appeal of the unknown."

There was no jealousy or resentment in his voice, just genuine worry, and she felt his concern. "Davis, don't worry. I know you're trying to take care of Peggy this summer, but there's no way you can be responsible for her feelings. You can't control whom she falls in love with, if that's what's happening."

"I guess not," he said moodily. "I just hate to see her hurt."

"Maybe she won't be," she said, trying to comfort him. Then she asked, "Did Peggy ask you whether you'd told Cody anything about her complaints?"

"Uh huh. I sort of got the feeling that her search for the answer to that question might have been the reason for the apology in the first place."

She chuckled. "I got the same feeling." She took a sip of soda. "But even if she's a bit transparent, I feel sorry for her. She dreads his knowing about her prejudice against him, but she knows she has to tell him about it pretty soon, before he hears it from someone else."

His eyes flashed to hers. "She does need to tell him. Any friendship's got to be based on honesty."

She looked back at him, absorbing the fact that he was putting an underlying significance into his words and his look. A flicker of her old anger came back. Was he talking about them? If so, he certainly had a lot of nerve. He was the one who'd been dishonest.

"Right," she answered dryly, refusing to pick up on any hidden meaning. "But now that she's attracted to him, it'll be really hard for her to tell him that she prejudged him. It'll be so painful for her if he doesn't understand."

He nodded. "For both of them. It would have been better if they'd never gotten together."

He stared past her for a minute, then he said, "Tracey, our friendship needs some additional honesty, too. We need to talk sometime while we're at Eldorado." His voice was low; its intimate tone shook her.

"No, we don't."

Her pulse throbbed in panic and anger, and she glanced away from him, out into the impersonal blue expanse of the sky. If she couldn't believe what his body had told her that night, if she couldn't trust that, then she couldn't believe anything he might tell her.

"There's something I need to explain to you," he said, speaking as carefully as if he were trying to gentle a wild thing.

When she spoke, fear of hurt and a deep resentment laced her voice. "Davis, let's just keep everything between us strictly business, okay? It'll be much better that way." Her tone sounded tight, brittle, even to her own ears.

"We can't," he said flatly. "I thought we already had a friendship going."

"I'd hardly call it that."

She was looking out the window again instead of at him, but she could feel him stiffen. The only sound was the engines as their pitch changed for the descent onto the private landing strip at the resort.

"Look at me, Tracey." His voice whipped at her, hard and relentless.

She didn't think she could meet his eyes without breaking into a thousand pieces, so she looked down at the table again, letting her hair swing to hide her face.

"Look at me," he growled again. The command held such authority that she had no choice. Finally she raised her eyes to his face.

"If you wouldn't call it a friendship, then what would you call it?" he demanded furiously, his steel blue eyes boring into hers. "We sure as hell have something more than a business relationship, whether you like it or not."

"Don't talk to me that way." Anger was beginning to pulse through her veins, growing stronger by the second, strong enough to overcome her hurt and her frustrated desire.

"That doesn't answer my question," he shot back.

She gazed into the iciness of his eyes, trying to

remain as calm as he seemed to be. "I thought we had a friendship going at one time, too," she told him. "But it turned out that to you it was nothing but an extension of business."

"What's that supposed to mean?"

She felt her cheeks flush with fury. "Don't pretend that you don't understand, Davis," she lashed out. "Don't add that little dishonesty to all the others." She stared into his eyes as if she were trying to read his mind. "Really, Davis, your saying that we need to be honest with each other is one of the most absolutely ironic things I've ever heard! I can't believe you'd have the gall to say that when you're the one who's been so *dis*honest!"

"Listen to me," he commanded furiously. "You tell me this minute how I've been dishonest with you! And what you meant with that crack about business!"

"I meant that I'm not living in my fantasy world anymore, Davis," she told him slowly, shaping every word with a cold surety. "You've been so wonderful in helping me see reality that I've finally woken up. I've become a practical person, just like you are, and now I see that you began our friendship, that you made love to me"— her voice almost faltered on those words but she forced it to stay steady—"only to try to stop my opposition to your policies at Southwest."

The sign telling them to fasten their seatbelts flashed. He stared into her eyes, astounded. He shook his head. "That isn't true," he said at last, his voice very deep and sure. "Tracey, you can't believe that."

"How can I not believe it when it's so obvious?" she

retorted. "It explains perfectly why you left me so abruptly with the announcement that there could be nothing permanent between us. You think we can't have anything lasting in our personal lives because we're so incompatible professionally, yet you're willing to have a temporary fling with me to try and shut me up for now."

She searched his face. "You even tried it again the other night at your house, telling me that you'd thought of the goodwill ambassador idea just to take some of the burden off me." She laughed sarcastically. "How very thoughtful of you, Davis. Presenting it to me that way should have kept me from fussing about the money, but somehow it just didn't work. Maybe that's because you've been giving me such good lessons about life in the real world."

He was listening to her with his entire being, watching her relentlessly and weighing every word. When she'd finished he kept holding her eyes with his until she began to read his look. There was no answering anger in it, just interest and determination and his usual complete self-assurance. That made her even angrier.

"You're absolutely wrong, Tracey," he said calmly. "I understand how you might have come to that conclusion, but you're wrong." He indicated the flashing sign. "We can't talk now, because we're about to land, but we'll get together tonight and I'll explain."

"We will *not* get together tonight!" she exclaimed, his arrogance feeding her rage. "And I don't want to hear any explanations. I can't believe anything you tell me, so I'll be spending my time on my work!"

She saw that that remark had struck home, and with a vague sense of satisfaction she turned away from him.

The plane bumped, then bumped again as it touched down. It rolled to a stop and the sound of the motors ceased.

She sat up very straight and unfastened her seat belt as the pilot came out of the cockpit.

"Here we are, folks, safe and sound," he said cheerfully. "The pleasures of Eldorado lie before you."

He opened the door and let down the steps.

Davis stood up, towering over her, his eyes slashing into hers. His jaw was set determinedly. "As I said, Tracey, sometime in the next couple of days we're going to talk. Right now I'll see you to the condominium, and then I have to go and find the senator."

His tone was so sure and so stubborn that she didn't answer. It was absolutely impossible to tell him anything, ever. She might as well stop trying and just wipe him right out of her mind. She stood, silently fuming, wanting nothing but to get away from him.

Outside, a young man driving a Jeep marked "Eldorado Resort" was waiting for them. "Turnbo Properties condominium, sir?" he asked as they got in.

"Right," Davis answered curtly.

They spoke very little on the short drive along the curving roads of the resort, and when the boy stopped at the door of the long glass and stone duplex Davis informed him abruptly that he'd take care of the luggage himself.

He unlocked a door, and after Tracey had stepped inside, he carried in her bags.

"I'll be staying in the other side of the condo," he said brusquely, handing her a key. "It has a separate entrance. Just call if you need anything."

He turned to go and she watched him leave. She couldn't wait until he was gone!

As he closed the door behind him, however, instead of relief she felt a sudden emptiness and doubt. He'd sounded so truthful when he'd told her that she was wrong about him. Was it possible? Had she misread him completely?

She pushed the thought away impatiently. If that were true, then she was more mixed up than ever. She didn't understand him at all.

She tossed her bag onto the low couch and walked restlessly to the long windows that faced west, unconsciously twisting the fragile gold chain she wore. This really *was* going to be a horrible weekend; not even the chance to lobby for money for the preserve would make her happy. She didn't care if she ever saw another white rhino, much less bought one. And it didn't help any to think about Dehli.

Or Peggy and Cody. She was happy for them, and she hoped that neither of them would be hurt, but every time she thought of their romance she was reminded of how she'd compared their relationship to hers and Davis's. If miracles were happening, then why couldn't one have happened for her, too?

Chapter Ten

Tracey tucked the last wisp of hair into the chignon at the nape of her neck. Then she slipped into a jade green silk dress, and while she fastened its tiny covered buttons she slowly turned around, surveying her appearance in the long mahogany-framed mirror in her dressing room.

Briefly the question of whether she'd misjudged Davis came into her mind again, and she castigated herself for the thought. It had haunted her during most of the sleepless hours when she hadn't been working on her speech, and part of the time when she had, but she couldn't think about it now. She hadn't seen or heard from him since the afternoon before, when he'd left her in her suite, and she was going to succeed in forgetting about him this morning.

She fastened two delicate gold chains around her

neck and applied her favorite lipstick. She had to push him out of her thoughts and concentrate on raising money for Southwest. She picked up a slim purse that matched her high-heeled sandals, checked to make sure it held her notes and left the room.

The large private dining room was crowded when she arrived; for a minute she stood in the doorway, trying to get her bearings. One wall of the room was glass, with plants hanging inside and out, and the morning light streaming through it shimmered off the white tablecloths and crystal vases.

The long head table was set up at one end of the room, and as she glanced that way Senator Martin caught her eye and signaled to her. He was serving as official host for the convention, and he and Mrs. Martin had been especially cordial to her at dinner the evening before. Now they were smiling at her, and he met her halfway across the room, taking her elbow as he escorted her to the chair beside his.

"We've been looking for you," he said. "My wife's been in a panic that we'd have to start without you."

"I'm glad you didn't," Tracey said. "I wouldn't want to miss anything."

"And we wouldn't want to miss your speech," Mrs. Martin said in greeting, leaning across her husband to speak to Tracey. "We're sorry you couldn't come to our party last night. We had a really good time."

"I'm sorry, too," Tracey answered sincerely. "But I did have to prepare for this morning."

The waiters began to serve ice cold melon and strawberries, and as she talked with the Martins,

Tracey's glance swept over the room. She didn't see Davis, and she concluded silently that he was missing this meeting just as he had the dinner meeting the evening before. Evidently he had made this trip to talk with Senator Crandall and that was all.

She could eat only a few bites of her Eggs Benedict, and though she took a tiny cinnamon roll from the basket in front of her, she hardly touched it. She was drinking her third cup of coffee when Senator Martin said, "I think it's about time, don't you?"

He went to the podium and made a few announcements; then he introduced Tracey as the featured speaker. It seemed to her that he was telling the entire story of her life, but at last he finished. She pushed back her chair and walked to the podium. She placed her notecards on it and looked up, ready to begin.

Davis was sitting at a table for four just to the right of the center of the room, directly in her line of vision. His clear blue eyes were fixed on her, and as she met them, he smiled his sexy smile and flashed her a tiny victory sign. Then he settled into his chair as if this speech were the only reason he'd come all the way from Tucson. He was ready to be entertained.

She gripped the edge of the podium with both hands, his glance tingling through her. He was still holding her gaze; she was powerless to stop him. She also was powerless to concentrate on anything but him.

How could she do this? she wondered frantically. How could she stand up in front of all these people and make a speech when she couldn't even think? Why couldn't he have skipped this meeting, too?

Panic flowed over her like a tide, and when it was gone a welcome numbness had taken its place. She tore her eyes away from him at last and let them move over the remainder of the crowd. Then she looked at the little white rectangles in front of her. She began to speak, not really knowing what she was saying, not hearing the sound of her own voice.

She regained consciousness when she realized that she was telling the story of Dehli; that was to be the end of her speech. She finished it, then briefly outlined the numbers and types of permits and other documentation that would be necessary to bring the elephant into the country. She summarized the rules and regulations of the transportation companies that handled the animals.

"Lately," she said, "those of us who work in zoos and wildlife preserves have a saying: 'When the weight of the paperwork required equals the weight of the animal, it's ready to be shipped.'" She waited until the polite laughter had subsided, and then concluded, "So, you see, you as legislators can be of tremendous help to us if you will make effective, yet simple laws concerning endangered species."

She was careful not to look in Davis's direction when she'd finished, and she welcomed the people who almost immediately surrounded her to ask questions. While she talked with legislators and people in businesses related to tourism who wanted to ask questions about Southwest, one part of her was hoping that he would leave, but another part was wishing desperately that he'd wait and speak to her.

At last she finished with all the questions and turned

to tell the Martins good-bye. As they left Davis spoke from behind her.

"You did a great job," he said in a conversational tone that suggested there'd never been an angry word between them. "All your worry was for nothing; you even made a hit with someone from Washington."

The low tones of his voice glimmered through her, and her hands trembled a little as she slid the stack of cards into her purse. "And who was that?" she asked.

"Senator Crandall. I was sitting with him, and he made several very positive comments."

They began to walk toward the door, and he took her arm. Immediately every cell in her body was sensitized only to him.

"The senator wants to meet you," he went on, "but he couldn't wait around just now. I asked him to come over to the condo later."

She stared up at him, sudden resentment mixing with the thrill she felt as his long fingers brushed her skin. One evening he'd ignored her as if she weren't even there, and then he made social plans for the next, as if they were sharing a room instead of staying in the adjoining halves of a condominium!

"You've made plans for me for this evening?" she asked frostily.

"Not with the senator. I suggested that he come over tomorrow sometime."

"What's that supposed to mean? That you're making plans for me *without* the senator?" Anger glittered in her voice and eyes.

"That's right. You go change while I make arrange-

ments for a car, and I'll pick you up in fifteen minutes."
He was still holding her arm, and he tried to guide her
toward the door, but she stood stock still. "Davis, you
expect me—"

"To wear a swimsuit," he interrupted. "And bring a
jacket. It gets cool on the water at night." Then he was
gone, the double glass doors swinging shut behind him.

She was going only because there was a chance that
she'd misjudged him, she told herself as she changed
into a strapless one-piece swimsuit. She slipped on
khaki shorts and a matching shirt over it. She owed it to
herself to find out.

She took her hair down from its chignon, then went
to find a headband to hold it out of her face in the wind.
His knock came in exactly the fifteen minutes he'd
promised, and she picked up her bag and the jacket that
matched her shorts as she went to the door.

He was wearing royal blue swim trunks, with a
matching shirt swinging open. The outfit made his eyes
look an even deeper blue and showed the wonderfully
muscular lines of his body. She was glad that she had
something in her hands; otherwise she probably
couldn't have kept them off him.

She looked away and put on her sunglasses, trying to
draw air into her lungs. They left the condo and walked
toward the same Jeep that had brought them from the
landing strip.

"Isn't a driver supposed to come with this thing?"
she asked.

"Yes, but I talked the manager out of it," he replied, his smile crinkling at her as he swung in behind the wheel. "He offered both the Jeep and a driver, since he didn't have a rental car available, but I told him that three people would definitely be too many on a trip like this." His voice held the sexy, intimate tone she loved.

But she wasn't going to give in to his fatal attraction again, she vowed as his words sank in. She was just going so she could hear whatever he had to tell her, and in the meantime she'd enjoy a real outing for the first time in the hectic weeks since Gerald had fallen ill. She looked around eagerly, drinking in the day as if she'd just awakened.

"So we're getting a new elephant," he remarked casually as they drove through the grounds of the resort in the direction of the highway. "You didn't mention that to me."

"I only found out yesterday," she answered. "It seems we have a benefactor in Phoenix we didn't even know we had."

"Bryan Shaw?"

She stopped trying to hold her hair in the wind so she could slip the headband on and stared up at him, her eyes wide with surprise. "How did you know? You just said you didn't know anything about it."

"No, I didn't. I said you didn't mention it to me." He grinned at her, his eyes full of mischief. "Bryan did."

"Davis!" she said, exasperated. "You are impossible!"

"And irresistible," he teased.

He was. At that moment, with his hair blowing across his forehead in the breeze, and his eyes happy and impossibly blue, he truly was irresistible. She caught a ragged breath, and when she let it go it carried with it all her fear of being with him.

She couldn't *not* be with him, she decided in that one translucent moment. If it were true that there could never be anything permanent between them, then there would have to be something temporary. It was impossible to exist in this wild countryside on this dazzling sun-filled morning and not be with him.

"But why are you so happy about this elephant?" he asked. "It's only one, not a whole herd, and I thought one of a kind is what you're always grousing about."

"But we'll have to breed her as soon as she's old enough," she explained, an exhilaration that had nothing to do with their newest acquisition running through her voice. "That's a prerequisite for getting an endangered female. We have to either have a male of the same species or show how we intend to breed her. There's a male at San Diego I think we can use."

"Then why are you always on my back about that rhino?" he asked. "Can't you do the same thing with him?"

"You're talking about two different species, Davis," she told him. "A male white rhino needs the stimulus of rival males around and enough females on hand to assure that some of them would come to him by choice. We can't really start a herd of our own any other way."

He nodded. "All right, I'll take your word for it."

"Well, it's about time! After all, I *am* the zoologist around here."

"And I'm the businessman," he retorted cheerfully. "And I've been working for your preserve, whether you think I have or not."

She looked questioningly at him as she got her hair under the headband at last.

He went on. "When Bryan Shaw called me about buying the elephant I thought of something. A twist for our public relations campaign. Why don't we appeal to local pride and the old spirit of the Southwest? If we'd begin an emphasis on native species, I think we could bring in a lot of donations."

She nodded enthusiastically. "That's a good idea. Of course we've established our ZooFriends Fund, but we haven't made a concerted effort to get large donations."

"Right. There are plenty of people in Arizona and all over the Southwest who could afford to make just as big a donation as Bryan is doing. And those who can't could make smaller contributions that we could combine."

"Do you mean bring cougars and wolves and bighorn sheep and maybe Wyoming's black-footed ferret into the preserve?"

"Yes. It doesn't really matter whether they're all threatened with extinction right now or not. With the way what we call civilization is moving, *every* wild thing will ultimately be a member of an endangered species."

She looked at him with a new respect; she'd had no

idea that he was that concerned about animals. But she should have known. After all, he had started Southwest in the first place.

"Tracey, a couple of weeks ago I saw a cougar on my ranch," he told her, his voice resonant with remembered excitement as he recalled the experience. "It was just roaming around free! I couldn't believe it—there are men who work in the wild who've never seen one in its natural habitat!"

His smile flashed at her. "It's a thrill that's indescribable, seeing an animal like that in the wild, fending for itself, going about its own business. Cougars are plentiful now, but we could build up a stock at Southwest that could be returned to the land if they should ever be endangered."

"You're right, Davis. And if we publicize our southwestern emphasis well, I really think we can get a lot more donations as large as Bryan Shaw's."

"Of course, I'm right," he affirmed. "And we're on our way to research some of these natives of the Southwest. I have a boat over on Lake Mohave, and we'll cruise Black Canyon and look for them."

"On a boat? We're going to look for the animals of the Southwest in a lake?"

"No, on the shores. I'm hoping we'll see bighorn sheep and some burros and maybe some herons." He looked away from the road and grinned at her. "You didn't come all the way up here just to stay in your room, did you? A zoologist couldn't come to a place this rich in wildlife and not even venture out to look at it!"

She laughed. "True," she murmured with mock thoughtfulness. "It would be a travesty."

"Exactly. That's the word I was searching for."

They turned onto Highway 93, and as they picked up speed conversation became difficult due to the noise of the wind and the engine. Tracey gave herself up to the wild beauty of her surroundings; the gray land dotted with the green of desert brush pulled at her, and the sun and wind exhilarated her. Their fierceness stirred her; they opened her senses, and she absorbed them until she felt as if she had become a part of the sun-drenched landscape.

They arrived at Willow Beach and a marina filled with boats of all sizes and kinds. Davis parked the Jeep near a rambling building, and as they got out a small white-haired man bustled through the door.

"Howdy, Mr. Turnbo," he called as he came over to them. "Ever'thing's all set." He raised one hand to shield his eyes from the sun and squinted up at Davis. "Mamie stocked up your food, and I filled 'er up and got you some firewood."

"Thanks, John."

"Gonna cruise Black Canyon, are you?" John asked. "May see some bighorn." He included Tracey in his keen glance. "Maybe a bunch of 'em. Man come in here last night said he seen a whole herd of 'em yesterday."

He was obviously willing to tell them more about the bighorn and probably a great many other subjects, but Davis took Tracey's elbow and tactfully edged them toward the boats.

"We're hoping to see some, and maybe some burros, too," he called back.

"Well, good luck to you." John lifted a hand in farewell, and they walked along the slip to board a highly polished navy blue and white cabin cruiser.

"What's all this about food and firewood?" she asked as they climbed onto the upper deck and Davis started the motors. "Sounds like a real expedition."

"It is," he answered teasingly. "Can't go on safari without supplies."

As the cruiser began to move out of the marina it seemed to Tracey that they were leaving the entire world behind. The shimmering blue water was a cool contrast to the heat of the desert sunshine, and a breeze played lightly in her hair. She stood close beside him, their arms barely touching as he held the wheel, and looked around with delight.

Towering cliffs loomed on both sides of the river, shadows playing over their bright colors to create an ever-changing panorama. Her eyes roamed over them, then to the water below, where the glistening surface caught the reflection of the mountains. She slipped the headband off and let her hair blow free.

They had gone only a short distance when a movement high on the bluff to the right caught her eye.

"Oh, Davis, look!" she exclaimed, taking his muscular arm in both her hands.

There were two bighorn sheep outlined against the light, and after that first movement they stood like statues, inherently bold and commanding against the indigo of the sky. They were exactly the same shades of gray, brown and white as the rocky ground beneath their hooves, and their magnificent horns curved starkly in the sun.

As Tracey and Davis watched, the sheep began to move, picking their way along the sheer mountain face with a sureness that made her gasp with admiration. They reached the top of a bluff and walked along it. Then, as her eyes strained to hold them, they climbed a ledge and at last were out of sight.

The sheep had been gone for at least a minute before either of them spoke. "Marvelous!" she breathed at last. "What a thrill to watch them! Especially when they're just 'going about their business,' as you said about your cougar."

He smiled down into her eyes, his lips curving sensuously. She held the look, loving it, wanting to prolong the moment of perfect empathy between them. He touched her face once, lightly, as if to say that he knew what she was thinking.

"I'm glad we're friends again," he murmured, his lips barely moving under his thick mustache.

She drank in the sight of him, wanting to touch him, wanting to walk into his arms, and she knew then that what he said was true. They *were* friends again, even without any explanations. She'd been wrong about him. She couldn't stand here in the breeze of this wonderful day and look into his eyes, blue as the lake beneath them, and not know that.

She wanted him.

And she loved him.

The thought beat against the sides of her mind like a caged bird that longed to fly free. She had a sudden, piercing desire to tell him what she'd just realized, to shout it to the desert wind that was blowing to them from the marvelous serenity of the quiet cliffs.

But she turned away instead and walked to the rail to try to understand it alone. She stood there for a long time as he guided the boat through the canyon, trying to absorb the wonder and the danger of it.

Finally they came around a sharp promontory formed by a high cliff, its reddish brown sides shining in the sun, reflecting in the clear water. There was a secluded cove on the other side of it, and Davis cut the motors, anchoring by the peaceful beach.

He turned to her, but his eyes went to her lips instead of meeting her glance. He didn't say anything for a minute. Then finally he looked into her eyes. "Let's swim for a while," he suggested. "I told you to wear your suit, so I'd better let you use it."

Before they climbed down onto the white sand of the beach he went below for the wood he'd mentioned, and for towels and a large, glen-plaid blanket. "We might as well start the fire before we swim," he said, handing her the towels and blanket to carry. "Then if the water gives us an appetite . . ."

His hands lingered on hers for a minute, and their languorous touch added to the smoldering in his eyes gave the unfinished sentence another meaning. Her heart lurched suddenly, hurtfully against her rib cage, and her hands shook a little as she took the things from him.

She shouldn't let this happen, she thought. Not until they had talked. Not until she knew his feelings.

But the love for him that she'd just recognized made her too vulnerable, and her traitorous body went limp with desire. She followed him off the boat and onto the sand.

He took off his loose shirt and dropped it onto the beach. His powerful shoulders tempted her; the tantalizing crispness of the hair on his chest made her palms tingle; the long strength of his thighs called to her as he walked around, exploring the beach and choosing the best place for the fire. Then he went back onto the cruiser for matches. When he returned she could look at nothing but him, and as he crouched beside the wood and deftly lit it the longing for him became intolerably strong and she had to move.

Her legs were aching with the desire to walk over to him, and her arms and hands prickled with the urge to explore his smoothly tanned back as he bent over the fire, but she fought the craving that was burning up her spine until at last she was able to look away.

She slipped out of her jacket, then her shirt and shorts, and dropped them beside the blanket. "I think I'll go on in," she said as she began walking toward the water.

He glanced up, and she saw the wanting flare in his eyes. They raked over her hungrily, embracing her all at once, and then they came back to explore her more slowly, moving from the swell of her breasts under the sleek fabric of her bronze-colored suit to her slender thighs.

He squinted up into her eyes. "Be with you in a minute," he told her gruffly.

She walked into the shallow water, and then began to swim once it became deeper. When she turned over onto her back the warmth of the sun made her face glow, but she was hardly aware of it. Her senses were attuned to Davis, and the memory of what he had once done to them was so strong that it blocked out everything else.

She turned over again and began to swim hard, searching for the distraction she'd hoped the water would provide, but she kept remembering everything about the night when they had made love, reliving every touch, every kiss. And her body was clamoring for more. It wasn't satisfied with physical activity, and it wasn't content with recollections from the past. It wanted Davis. Now. Nothing, no one, else.

She swam in a shallow circle and then headed back toward the beach, needing to see him, to touch him before another second passed. Just as she shook the water out of her eyes to search for him, he stood up. Her breathing sped up, then slowed as he stooped again to make one last adjustment to the fire. Then he started walking into the water, and her breathing seemed to stop altogether. He was coming to her!

She began swimming toward him as naturally as if he'd called to her, and when they met there was no need for words. He reached out to cradle her head and pull her lips to his as if not even one day had passed since he'd made love to her. She responded, offering her mouth to him as if it was his by right.

His kiss was sensual proof of the craving for her that had been in his eyes; his lips took hers voraciously, and as hers parted under them, his tongue thrust into her mouth. He explored every inch of it, stroking it yearningly, exciting her until she was dizzy. Urgently she kissed him back, encouraging him, begging him with her tongue to continue, to give her again all the overpowering sensations she had missed for so long.

His hands were on her then, exploring her body as his tongue was exploring her mouth. Slowly, sensuously, they moved over her through the water of the lake. They caressed her waist, then the neat curve of her hips.

She moved her legs to stay afloat, and he pulled her over, leaning her into him as he began to drift on top of the water. Without breaking the kiss he began running his hard hand over one of her long thighs, rubbing and stroking it, stopping to investigate the high vee cut legs of her suit with his fingers as his eyes had done on the beach. He touched her just under the edge of it once, lightly, then he traced the sensitive skin all around the shape of it. Her whole body trembled, even on the inside, from the magic his fingers were creating.

She ran one hand over his back and down to his hips in response. He broke the kiss with a gasp, and she opened her eyes to look at him. His face beneath the droplets of crystal water was handsome enough to break her heart.

"Let's get back to the beach," he muttered huskily. "But don't you leave me for a minute."

His lips claimed hers again, and they half floated, half swam to shore, a tangle of arms and legs, unable to stop touching each other, helpless to break the kiss. As they fell onto the warm sand of the beach neither of them was able to think of, much less look for, the blanket.

She sank into the sand, as unaware of its slight roughness as she was of its warmth. Davis was the only source of heat for her.

"Tracey, I have to look at you," he groaned as he tore his lips from hers. "Let me see you; let me touch you."

He pulled her suit down and away from her wet body quickly, almost roughly, and his gaze followed it as if his eyes were tearing the concealing fabric away, sweeping down the length of her. "You're so beautiful," he marveled, his gaze coming back to her face. "You're the most beautiful woman I've ever known."

"Oh, Davis, I've needed you so," she cried in response, and his eyes moved away from hers to the smooth white mounds of her breasts.

He moaned and bent to take the rosy tip of one of them into his mouth. His teeth and his tongue around it created pure delight, and the feelings that radiated through her from that one point changed her thoughts and her words to the present. "I need you, Davis; I need you. Davis, make love to me."

She reached for the waistband of his swimsuit and pushed at it, but she was so weak from the onslaught of his mouth as it went from one of her breasts to the other, and so unwilling to risk losing that pleasure even for an instant, that she couldn't seem to function. She ran her hands over his hips and whimpered with frustration at the fabric between her skin and his.

At last he moved away enough to take it off. "No," she murmured, frustration making the word almost a cry. "Come back. . . ."

But when he did come back to her after seconds that seemed like hours he lay beside her just for a moment, his leg barely touching her, but not his hands or his mouth.

She opened her eyes to find him again. His smoldering gaze was devouring her. Then, with the utmost confidence, he put one hand flat against her stomach as if he were claiming her as his.

She gasped with the sharp gratification of it and reached for him with the same sense of possessiveness. He came into her arms and moved over her, the weight of his body deliciously heavy and marvelously stimulating.

He moved against her just once, and for the space of a heartbeat everything stopped except for the exquisite torment bursting through her veins.

She was tracing his earlobe with her tongue, but she stopped and ran it along his cheek and over his mustache to his lips instead, wanting his mouth on hers as he entered her.

His mouth opened to her as she did to him, and they joined together then. They moved wildly, passionately, in a cadence created by the sexuality that had been undulating between them since their first fervent glance.

That rhythm, that melody, caught her up and obliterated her, absorbing all of her into its inexorable beat until she was not herself any longer. She was a part of its song, and she was a part of Davis, a new being who lived only to feel him inside her, to hold his miraculous body in her arms.

Their passion built and built until it reached its zenith, and at that incredible instant of fulfillment the wonder of it made her whole again. Her love for him filled her to overflowing, and she thought that she would burst with it if she couldn't tell him how she felt.

But he spoke, and for a second that seemed as long as an age she couldn't believe that it was his voice and not her own that she had heard.

"I love you," he said. "Tracey, I love you."

Chapter Eleven

*H*is quiet words stopped her heart entirely. Joy poured through her as she absorbed the import of what he'd said. He loved her, too! She smiled, glowing up at him with the delight of that revelation added to the sensuous aftermath of their lovemaking.

The curve of his lips and the lazy pleasure in his eyes told her that he hadn't forgotten one second of what had just passed between them, either. But there was something else in his look, too: a cloud of doubt. Then the words, "Tracey, I love you," played themselves again in her mind, and for the first time she was aware of their tone. A warning bell went off in her brain, and fear tempered her gladness.

"Davis, what is it?" she asked, reaching out to touch his cheek.

"Tracey, I have to tell you about Marla," he said

slowly, his voice very low. His eyes caressed hers, begging her to understand why another woman's name was on his lips at a moment like this.

"All right," she said softly. She waited for him to go on, but he didn't. Finally she questioned, "Davis?"

He started to answer, then restlessly, abruptly, he sat up and moved away from her, reaching for his clothing. "Let's not waste the fire," he said harshly, regretfully, as if he wished that he hadn't brought up the subject at all. "I'll tell you while we make dinner."

The sun was sliding lower now; his words and the distance he'd put between them let the coolness that was creeping into the air chill their sweat-dampened bodies. With his warmth removed from her, she was cold. She sat up, too, and found her clothes.

"Let me help," she said quietly. "Tell me what to do."

"Just sit right there where I can see you. Don't do anything but listen. I want to tell you this, but it'll take me a minute. It hurts like hell."

He set up the little grill, then left her to go to the cruiser for a picnic basket and the specially seasoned hamburger meat and corn in the husk that Mamie had prepared. Once the food was cooking he began again.

"This is what I've been trying to tell you," he said, searching her face. His eyes were dark, almost black in the shadows. "I've needed to tell you, really, ever since the first time I saw you."

His eyes left hers and sought the fire. "I was married to her for three years, and no matter what I did I could never make her happy." His lips barely moved as he spoke; his voice was subdued. His whole body was unnaturally still, still with the hurt of opening an old wound.

He stared into the flames for an endless moment; then his eyes came back to hers. "She was killed in an automobile accident and it was my fault."

"Oh, Davis." She stared at him, not moving, numbed by the pain in his voice and his body.

"It's been five years, and it still haunts me every day."

"Davis, I'm so sorry," she said gently. "Were you driving?"

"No. She was alone in the car."

"Then how could? . . ."

"How could it be my fault?" His tone roughened. "Because she was running away from an argument with me. We were having one of our constant quarrels, and she got so upset that she rushed out into a raging thunderstorm. A few miles out of Tucson she hit a guard rail and the car flipped over the side of a canyon. She died instantly."

"Davis, you can't take the responsibility for that," she told him, trying with the intensity of her eyes and her voice to take away some of the hurt that was filling him, wanting but not daring to go to him and try to banish it with her arms and lips. "You can't blame yourself. *She* made the decision to leave the house in the storm."

He poked at the fire, negating her words with a shake of his head. "But if our marriage had been good, it wouldn't have happened," he said, his voice empty and flat. "I gave her everything I could give, but it wasn't enough. I could never make her happy. I failed her."

"You can't *make* somebody else happy, Davis, not even in marriage. We all discover in our own way how to be happy."

"But Marla . . . somehow Marla *couldn't* learn how by herself; she needed me to help her. And God knows I tried. I tried everything I knew, but it didn't do any good." The words rolled out of him with practiced ease, and she knew that he'd said them to himself a thousand times.

"These things are inexplicable, Davis," she said. "Just as a lot of things about life are. I tried and tried for years, but I never understood why my parents had to die when I was so young, or why my aunt who raised me couldn't have loved me enough to devote some time to me."

"But you were a child; you weren't responsible."

"I thought I was. Somehow I felt it was all my fault that no one loved me, and for a long time that affected my adult relationships." She reached for his hand. "Maybe there was something like that in Marla's background, something deeply rooted that made her so desolate, something she simply had to work through by herself."

He didn't respond to her touch; he merely shrugged skeptically. She knew that he'd heard *those* words a thousand times, too.

"Maybe," he mumbled.

"Davis, didn't you tell me one time that during your

childhood you took your responsibilities as the big brother very seriously?"

Startled, he glanced up to meet her eyes. "Yes."

"Well, maybe that habit is still affecting your thinking," she said softly. "You believe that you should have single-handedly been able to make Marla a happy person; you're worrying that somehow you need to look out for Peggy's emotions. It could be, you know, that you're doing the same thing I did when I was a child: You're taking responsibility that really isn't yours to take."

He looked at her for a long time, searching her face as if to find an answer as to whether that speculation was fact or not, and then slowly he said, "I don't know. I've never really thought of it that way." He shrugged again, an unspeakably weary movement. "I'm just used to being in control, to doing whatever I set out to do, to accomplishing whatever I want."

Slanting rays from the lowering sun played on the hard angles of his face. "But when it comes to a deep relationship with a woman I can't seem to do that. That's one area where I can't succeed at all."

"But that's not an area where the same rules apply, you know," she said quietly. "Relationships are a joint endeavor."

He appeared not to hear her. "Anyway, Tracey, I wanted you to know that I walked away from you because of Marla. Not because of you. I can't ever commit myself to anyone else, and it's only fair that you know that."

She looked back at him silently, her emotions careening from love to compassion to despair.

"And that's why I should never have made love to you. It just makes me want you more, over and over again."

"And why shouldn't you want me?" she asked at last, her words very quiet in the still night air.

"Because it makes me want you forever," he said, just as softly. "And that isn't fair to you. I wasn't going to let myself love you, but I do. Tracey, I love you more than I ever loved Marla, and I couldn't live with it if I failed you, too."

"But, Davis . . ."

He shook his head and stood up restively, brushing her words away with a sharp gesture. "I don't want to talk about it any more right now," he said, his tone as rough as it had been soft only seconds before. "Let's have dinner."

She filled their plates as he opened the basket and poured them each a glass of burgundy, and they settled side by side onto the blanket.

Neither of them ate very much, though; emotions were running too strongly inside them. Thoughts beat around in her head like frantic birds' wings; she was desperate to explore the issue with him, to make him talk and listen until they'd exorcised the demons that were darkening his eyes to a midnight blue and cutting deep creases of worry into his chiseled face.

She needed to convince him that it couldn't possibly have been all his fault that Marla had died. And she longed to tell him that if they were committed to each other, he wouldn't fail her. But he was closed to her now. It had hurt him too much to open up; he was back inside his protective shell.

Finally they gave up the pretense of eating and watched the line of shadow on the orange cliff across from them rise higher and higher until the only light left was that of their fire. Outside its circle the dark lake and the mountains beyond seemed very far away.

He was motionless, silent, and the firelight fell across his face. She ached to touch his features, to smooth the agony away.

Instead she took a handful of sand and let it run through her fingers; it was no longer white, but a purple blue in the darkness. "I know it's hard to forget," she said at last. "But, Davis, you have to live again."

He turned to look at her, and she couldn't go any farther. His eyes were filled with the anguish twisting in him, the war of wanting her and not letting himself have her. She reached up to his face, cupping it in her hands, running one thumb along his cheekbone. "Davis, I love you, too," she murmured, raising her lips to him. "I love you, too."

A new expression, a gladness, flared behind the misery in his eyes. It suffused his face for a moment, but she could see him fighting it, trying to keep it from making the battle he lived with even more difficult. He didn't move, though their lips were a breath apart.

For the space of a heartbeat he resisted. Then at last he moved, slipping one of his strong hands into her wind-tousled hair. Their lips met with a joy that defied the sadness they'd just shared, with an elation that sprang from the same deep life-source that had woven the magic closeness around them all during the day. They parted and touched again, lightly, eagerly, quickly, everywhere at once, yet almost hesitantly, as if it were the very first time they'd joined together.

She'd begun the kiss to make him come back to life, but instead he was pouring the soul into her. The dynamic force of it was making her senses reel.

His hand went under her shirt to spread its warmth over her bare back. He molded his palm to her skin, tracing its silky contours from her delicate shoulder blades down the narrow valley of her spine.

She trembled under his touch, and her lips parted against his cheek, her tongue darting out to tempt him, to draw his mouth away from the kisses he was scattering on her cheekbones, her eyelids, her hairline. His lips came obediently to her mouth and took hers in a way that proved beyond a doubt that the two of them could, indeed, create life; his tongue hungrily searched out every bit of her sweetness.

Her tongue played with his—at first with the high-spirited excitement of the moment before, deliciously teasing him; then it entwined with his and became seriously provocative. He moaned and pulled her to him in a rough movement of need, pressing her breasts against the hard muscles of his chest.

Impatient with the thick fabric of her jacket against his bare skin, he pulled back and, his lips still holding hers, opened it and slipped it off her shoulders. He caressed the long smoothness of her arms as if to compensate her for the loss of warmth, and then his fingers reached for the buttons of her blouse.

His lips and his tongue continued their demands, continued to lay an exciting claim to her. She clasped his broad shoulders and pulled him to her, the tips of her fingers digging into his flesh with the same message his lips were giving hers.

When she was dizzy with the seduction of it, with the intimations of ecstasies to come, when she had floated in his power until she had forgotten how to breathe, even that she needed to breathe, his lips left hers and moved to the sensitive spot at the side of her neck. He nibbled and teased at her ear while he slowly opened one button of her blouse, then another and another.

His breath was hot against her ear and in the curve of her neck; his fingers were scorching the skin between her breasts. She wasn't even aware of the cool night air that he was letting in to touch her; the heat of him canceled all the coldness in the world.

His lips trailed along her collarbone and down the center of her throat to follow the path that his fingers had traced. They clung to her skin; they became a part of it, and his tongue left its mark each time it touched. She shivered with the delicious sensations that he was creating, and when he worked his way to the swollen tip of her breast and took it between his teeth she uttered a wordless cry.

Her fingers dove into his hair and tangled in it; she held his head to her as fiercely and as delicately as if her very life depended on keeping them in exactly that position, on preserving that thrumming note of bliss that was singing in her ears and vibrating in every cell of her body.

He let her nipple go at last, and his lips moved back to kiss her mouth before they slowly traveled again down the path she felt was burned forever into her silken skin and found her other breast. An intoxicating thrill surged through her, and she arched needfully toward him, murmuring his name over and over again.

His hands traced her sides and the curve of her waist, and slipped over the roundness of her hips. Vaguely she was aware that he was removing the rest of their clothing, but her head was spinning and her blood was pounding in her veins with such urgency that she was unaware of specific facts. Everything—his hands, his lips, his tongue, the hard length of his body against hers—blended together with the open spaces and the enfolding night to carry her away from any reality but him.

"Davis . . ." she whispered, the sound low and tentative, almost a question. Then she moved to touch him in return, to luxuriate in his muscular, masculine form, in the strong perfection of him. She stroked the long roundness of his thighs, reveling in their sinewy lines, running her hands possessively over every inch of him as if in that way she could make him belong totally to her.

He entwined his legs with hers then, and she shivered with delight as his fingertips moved over her back and his palms cupped the roundness of her hips. "Tracey," he rasped, his breath warm and fragrant against her mouth, "this has been a perfect day. I'll never forget it as long as I live."

"Neither will I," she murmured as she twined her arms around his neck and turned her face to ask for his lips again. "Oh, Davis, neither will I."

When they broke apart at last she began to imitate what he'd done to her, trailing kisses over the strong column of his neck and down onto the roughness of his chest. He growled her name and forced a shuddering breath into his lungs, and she felt his hard strength against her.

She smiled, excitement racing through her at being able to arouse him so. She arched up to him and, her breasts pressing into the hardness of his chest, caught the lobe of his ear with her teeth. She teased it with both her teeth and her tongue, and he wrapped her even tighter in his arms.

She began to build the tension, to nurture it, running the tips of her fingers over his back, his hips and the backs of his thighs, at first drawing wild patterns and designs, then smaller and smaller concentric circles at the base of his spine until he shivered with passion.

Finally she aroused him to the point of no return, and he rolled her over onto her back, his hard length on top of her, pressing her into the soft cradle of the sand. He moved against her lightly, teasingly, tantalizingly. "This is what you get, you little vixen," he said huskily. "I'm going to pay you back for driving me to distraction."

He pulled back, and for a long, pulsing moment the crisp mat of hair on his chest rubbed against the peaks of her breasts while his mouth tasted hers. The ecstatic torment of the two sensations poured into her and through her, causing the ground beneath her to rock crazily. His lips drew the very heart from her; they took her breath, her will, her thoughts; they left nothing at all for her except the warm sorcery of his body.

She tore her mouth from his; she had to speak to him or she would die. "Oh, Davis, Davis, make love to me," she gasped, her voice almost inaudible.

He moved back and held himself above her for a long minute that tortured her with waiting. She looked up into his eyes, shadowed in the flickering of the fire, then finally pulled him down to her, unable to resist her boundless desire for him.

Her lips parted; she had to tell him something else, but she couldn't remember what it was. At last she gave up; she was beyond speech.

When he entered her it stilled not only her words, but her very breath for an eternal instant. For another second he stared deeply into her eyes. Then his heavy lids closed slowly, sensuously, and when he found her mouth again with his the delectably slow rhythm of his tongue matched the erotic rhythm of their passion.

She wrapped her arms and legs around him to close the last fraction of distance between them, and they moved together into a new existence. The need he built in her was greater than she'd ever thought it could be. It spun in her and through her, tightening in her very center and spiraling, drawing her wildly up and up until she felt that she would die of it. She clung to him in desperation, moving with him in perfect unison, crying out his name until the dizzying end rushed over her.

He held her savagely close as her tremors of pleasure gradually subsided, and she felt his fierce fulfillment at having given her such satisfaction. Then he let himself go and she held his arching body, an answering happiness surging through her.

After that they didn't move until the last shuddering remnants of sweet sensation had died away. They lay for a long time, totally spent. She was folded in his embrace, her head cradled in the refuge of his shoulder, and she couldn't imagine ever wanting to be anyplace else. After a few minutes his breathing slowed, then slowed some more. He was asleep, one arm still clutching her to him.

Gradually she became aware of her surroundings for the first time since she'd reached out to him, and she gazed up at the stars. She shivered a little and pulled the blanket up and around them both like a cocoon, welcoming its rough warmth against her skin, hating the thought that had just come to her. Davis might be wrapped in her arms there at the edge of the fire, but he was also as far away from her as those stars.

Chapter Twelve

Tracey squinted into the sun and peered around the truck ahead of her as she headed east on Highway 86 toward Southwest. Some coffee from her mug splashed onto her hand as she pulled out to pass, and she knew that her eyes were grainy from lack of sleep, but she was oblivious to physical discomfort. Davis loved her, and while she was thinking about that nothing else could really penetrate her consciousness.

She'd been sealing out every other realization since that moment on the beach when she'd admitted to herself just how much stood between them. For the remainder of the time they'd been at Eldorado they hadn't spoken again of either the past or the future; they'd existed only in the present, reveling in being together, luxuriating in a world of the senses that held no room for words or regrets.

The marvelous closeness had still enclosed them when the Lear jet touched down at Mesa Field well after midnight, and she wasn't yet free of its spell. She parked her little Datsun in its usual place and, gathering up her purse and papers, abstractedly made her way through the halls toward her office.

Lottie wasn't at her desk, and Tracey glanced at her watch, wondering whether she'd somehow arrived terribly early. It assured her that it was almost nine o'clock, however, and Gerald's voice floating out from his office reinforced the fact that it was time to go to work. She was crossing the reception area to her own door when she became aware of what he was saying.

"I just don't know, Ken; that's a good price, but even at a bargain, rhinos take a chunk out of a budget."

There was silence for a long moment, then Gerald's voice again. "Well, I'll talk it over with the people on the board and get back to you. Thanks for calling."

She put her things on her desk and went straight into his office. "Hi, Gerald," she greeted him happily. "Am I one of the people you're going to talk it over with?"

He looked up from doodling on his blotter, his smile warm and welcoming. "So you're back from Eldorado," he greeted her. "And you seem to have survived all in one piece. Sit down and tell me all about it."

All about it. She felt the warmth rise to her cheeks as she thought of Davis and everything they'd shared.

"All right, but I want to know about your phone call first," she evaded. "I overheard the word 'rhinos.'"

He smiled and shook his head in pretended disgust. "Don't you know the saying about eavesdroppers?"

"Yes, but I've never believed a word of it. Now, what's going on?"

He sighed theatrically and gave in. "Fairmont Zoo has four, three cows and one bull, that they'd like to get rid of. They aren't doing well; Ken says they simply don't have enough room for them, and he thought we might like to buy them since we have Maqu."

"Wonderful!" she exclaimed. "Is the price awfully high?"

"Not nearly so high as it could be. To be perfectly honest, they're a bargain."

"Oh, Gerald! Do you think we can buy them?"

He smiled at her. "We're certainly going to try. Let's both go to the board meeting tonight and give it our best shot."

She hadn't even known that there was going to *be* a board meeting. She'd see Davis! For a second that thought blotted out everything else, even her excitement over the precious rhinos.

She forced her mind away from Davis, however, and she and Gerald talked about the possibility of the purchase for several minutes more. She reported to him on her speech and the contacts she'd made at Eldorado, then told him about Davis's idea to use a "Pride in the Southwest" theme for the public relations campaign. After that she went to her own office to try to get started on the day's regularly scheduled chores. Gerald had assured her that he would go home at noon and rest until the board meeting, so she wanted to finish her own work during the morning and concentrate on taking his place that afternoon. He just *had* to be able to come to the meeting; this might be the last chance in a long time to buy some companions for Maqu!

But once she was seated at her desk, her work spread out before her, she found that there was no way she could concentrate. She swiveled her chair so that she could look out onto the lawns that surrounded the building, images and emotions from the weekend whirling through her brain. The marvelous surge of joy was still there whenever she relived Davis's saying, "Tracey, I love you." For a timeless moment she sat there, thrilling again in every cell of her body to the memories of all the ways he had touched her.

She stared at the groups of visitors who were beginning to crowd the paths between the exhibits, exploring the zoo before the day became unbearably hot, but she saw none of them. She went over in her mind every word that had passed between her and Davis, every nuance of feeling during the entire time they'd been together. He loved her! Those words were still obliterating everything else that he'd said to her, and everything else in her life.

By the time the board meeting was over that evening she felt as if she'd been torn into two different people. She'd argued eloquently for the purchase of the Fairmont rhinos, and on one level she'd been elated when the board had approved using a percentage of the public relations campaign donations for them, but from the moment that Davis had come into the room every one of her five senses had been clamoring to be closer to him, to touch him. Now people were leaving, and in a few minutes they could be alone at last.

She and Gerald congratulated each other on their partial victory, and he assured her that he thought the public relations campaign would bring in sufficient donations. They chatted for a few minutes while Davis was finishing a conversation with Bud Mattson and another board member; then Gerald finally said good-bye and left, and Mattson and the other man walked out with him. Davis walked quickly toward her.

She waited for him without moving, and their eyes devoured each other as if they'd been separated for years. For an endless minute they stood, oblivious to everyone around them, communicating with no need at all for words.

"Let's go outside," he suggested at last. "It's a beautiful night."

They left the building and began to walk slowly along the gravel path into the African Savanna Exhibit, enveloped in each other and in the quietness of the night. The zoo seemed strange, empty of visitors and dark; there were only the quarter moon and a scattering of stars for light. Occasionally the trumpet of an elephant rang out, but the silence remained essentially unbroken.

She was still feeling much more than she was thinking. It felt so good simply to be beside him; it seemed years since she'd left him at Mesa Field.

But he didn't touch her, even though they were walking very close together, and he didn't refer to their weekend at all. He made a few general remarks about the meeting, and finally he began to talk in a desultory way about the zoo and the funding for the rhinos. She thought about it and was amazed that something that had once been so important to her suddenly could be of so little interest. She simply could *not* think about work, and she certainly didn't want to talk about it.

She wanted to talk about them, about their relationship. She wanted him to tell her again that he loved her. She wanted him to say it over and over so that the sound of it would drown out the tiny voice in the back of her mind that was trying to remind her that he'd also told her he'd never make another commitment to a woman.

She needed to feel his arms around her again to blot out that realization she'd had under the stars. He just couldn't be that far away from her!

She shook her hair back from her face and looked up at him. Why was she thinking about that now? She hadn't let herself remember once since, but now, without warning, she was having that despairing feeling again.

"Here's an idea I had," he was saying, and she tried to listen to his words and not to the remote quality that was creeping into his voice. "To begin the campaign to emphasize the native species exhibit, why don't we have Cody and Peggy work together and show Sand at her speeches and other appearances?"

She nodded. "It sounds good. But I'm surprised that you'd want to throw them together that much, since you're concerned about their relationship."

He raised one sandy-colored brow in rueful surrender. "You were probably right in saying that Peggy's love life isn't my responsibility. Anyway, from what she told me today they're together all the time anyway. They might as well be working."

She chuckled. "Slave driver! All right. That'll work out very well, because I don't think Peggy's ever going to handle animals well on her own. Cody's wonderful with Sand, and he'll be good with the other animals, too." She tried to focus her full attention on the idea. "Also, we have to do something really exciting in public relations right now, since their success will determine whether or not we get the rhinos!"

"True," he agreed. "Now, the other thing we need to talk about is the snow leopard exhibit."

And us, she added silently. And us.

"We've let this go too long now; John Grant called me this afternoon to ask for a projected completion date."

"Good heavens!" she burst out impatiently, her nerves tightening with this continual talk of business. "Doesn't he know that we couldn't possibly know that now?"

"I tried to tell him that, but he wasn't too understanding," he said. "I thought maybe tonight we could at least get started."

Was *that* why he'd suggested this walk? That wasn't what his eyes had said inside the conference room.

"I guess the first thing we need to talk about is the design for the enclosure and what kind of wire to use."

"Wire! I thought we'd build a grotto!"

They were in front of a little bench, and he stopped. He touched her, but not in a way she expected. He took her shoulders in his big hands and turned her to face him, his grip firm and almost punishing; she had the sudden feeling that he'd like to shake her.

"Tracey, you know better than that!" he burst out. "No one, I mean *no one,* has enough money to buy the concrete for that. An animal that can jump that far would require an *enormous—*"

"Don't lecture me," she snapped, desperate for his hands to be loving, not cruel. "I know all about how far snow leopards can leap. But I also know what kind of preserve I want us to have here, and what kind of display zoo. I *hate* seeing the animals in cages!"

He stared down at her for a long while, his steely fingers biting into her shoulders, his lips curved in a sadly rueful smile. She stared back, trying to read the succession of emotions that were chasing each other across his face.

"Tracey . . ."

But he couldn't finish the sentence. He reached for her, hungrily, desperately, and pulled her into his arms with a sound deep in his throat that was half-sigh, half-moan. He wrapped her in his arms and held her close, his face buried in her hair.

"I've thought about nothing but you since I left you at the airport," he murmured brokenly. "I tried to sleep after I got home, and I've tried to work today, but all I can do is think about you."

"I've been the same way, Davis," she whispered. "You're in my thoughts so much it's as if you're actually with me everywhere I go."

His strong arms tightened around her even more, and as she drank in the warmth of his musky, masculine fragrance she forgot the expression that had just suffused his face, the look that she didn't understand.

This was what she'd been expecting when they walked outside the building; *this* was what she'd been craving since the minute they'd parted at the airport. Her feelings for him ran incredibly deep, she realized now; at this moment she was boundlessly happy to be with him.

She was feeling the sharp stirrings of passion that he always created in her, but now there was something else just as powerful running underneath. It was a feeling of security. She was depending on him. She loved him, and he loved her, too, and that made her feel secure for the first time in years.

She hadn't felt this way since she'd become engaged to Eric, and not at all since he'd broken their engagement and left her completely alone again. And this was even more intense. She loved Davis much more than she'd ever loved Eric; this feeling of being connected to him went straight to the roots of her being.

She lifted her face to his, letting this new realization shine in her eyes and show in her smile. An answering smile was on his lips, but his eyes were in shadow. She stopped trying to see into them as his mouth came down to hers, and as his warm lips took hers and began to stroke and caress them, she stopped thinking entirely and parted her lips to him, taking him to her as if she were sure that they'd never have to be apart again.

His tongue tasted her mouth as if he'd been starving for her, and his lips pressed hers with a bruisingly fierce need. Her hands caressed the magnificent strength of his neck, of his broad shoulders. Then her fingers danced through his hair, pulling his mouth even harder against hers.

Mindlessly she floated into the sensual world they alone could share, unable to imagine that there could ever be anything else that she would want or need.

He cupped her to him, pressing her hips to his. Then, his strong thighs holding her securely against him, his hands began to roam the delicate contours of her back, wandering to her sides and up to her full breasts. She moaned as the now wonderfully familiar excitement spread through her.

She felt him tense a little at the sound she made, but he was as powerless as she was to stop the kiss; it carried both of them on a wave of sensation that in itself was a complete act of love. It told her that he loved her just as his words had done on the beach, and that was all she'd ever need to know.

Finally, sated, he broke the kiss and cradled her even more tightly in his arms, her head tucked against his chest. "Oh, Tracey," he murmured, his voice raw with the magnitude of the emotions tearing at him. "We'll be all right. If we can just take it one day at a time . . ."

At first the words played in the air above her head, not touching her, but then they battered their way into her brain and reverberated there. One day at a time!

But she was thinking about forever! How could he kiss her that way and then say "we can just take it one day at a time?"

Pain burst with a blinding brilliance in her heart. He *didn't* love her, not as she understood love. Those words had been a lie. That kiss had been a lie.

She couldn't depend on him. He didn't want to be close to her forever any more than her aunt or Eric had. But she couldn't take any more temporary relationships, especially not one with him. Her feelings for him went too deep; she knew that with an instinct as old as life itself.

She forced him away with a strength she didn't know she had, with a violence born of the savage flames of hurt and anger that were licking along every nerve ending in her body. "Leave me alone!" she cried, the words catching in her throat. "I want forever with you, and if you don't feel that way, too, then I don't ever want to see you again!"

She turned and ran from him down the path back toward her car. She had to get away from him; she had to be alone to try to find a way to staunch the hurt pouring from the gaping wound he'd torn in her heart.

Davis slammed his body into the driver's seat of the Ferrari and turned the key. As soon as the motor roared to life he gunned it and peeled out of the parking lot with a speed that made the car shudder.

It was a good thing he was in this car tonight, he thought fiercely. If there'd ever been a time when he needed the seductive escape of pure speed, this was it. He had to have the thrill of moving faster and faster through the desert night, the sense of moving like a comet over the surface of the earth. It would take that, at least, to help him bear this agony.

He managed to stop at the intersection of the main driveway and the highway; then he sped out onto the pavement with a squeal of his tires that pierced the night. The wind whipped his hair more and more strongly as his velocity increased, and as the force pulled him into a curve the thought came to him that if he kept pressing down on the accelerator the way he was doing he might well roll the car over.

He didn't care, he thought savagely. Maybe that would be for the best. At least it would put him out of his misery.

Damn it! *Why* had he just stood there and let her go? Why hadn't he called out to her, run after her, brought her back into the circle of his arms where she belonged?

Because she was such a hopeless dreamer, that was why. He couldn't give her a grotto for the snow leopards, or a dozen white rhinos. He couldn't make all her fantasies into realities with a sweep of his hand.

And she didn't want to try it one day at a time.

With her it was all or nothing, and he'd known that from the moment he'd looked into her enormous amber eyes. And now that he knew something of her background it was doubly true. She needed to feel permanently loved.

The rending pain that had been in her voice as she

cried out to him rang in his ears over the rumble of the powerful engine, and unconsciously he pushed down even harder on the accelerator. He couldn't stand to think how he'd hurt her: first her face at the office that night, then her eyes on the beach when he'd told her about Marla and his doubts about commitment, and now the raw despair of her voice echoing across the eerie quiet of the zoo's gardens.

The potent beam of his headlights picked up the sign, "Santa Rosa——5," and instinctively he started to slow for the turn. He could take that road and go straight to her house; he could find her, take her in his arms again, try to erase the hurt he'd caused.

Then, viciously, his foot descended. He couldn't go to her. Not now. Not yet. Maybe not ever. She was right. If he couldn't tell her that they could be together forever, he had no right to speak to her at all.

Tracey made no attempt whatsoever to sleep. She went straight into her house without even a pat for Geoffrey and ripped her clothes from her body. She stepped into a pair of worn jeans and pulled a soft cotton top over her head, then slammed back out and headed for the stable. Foxfire nickered at the sound of the door, and by the time Tracey reached her she was standing with her ears up, eager for company.

Tracey bridled and saddled her, then swung up on the mare's back with a determination born of despair. She had to make herself feel something else—the rhythmic movements of the big mare under her, the night breeze in her hair, the cool air against her face—*something* else besides the terrible wracking pain that was ripping her into shreds.

She bent over to unfasten the gate that would let them out of the corral; then she leaned over the horse's neck and gave her her head. The stars were brighter now, and she could see the terrain beneath Foxfire's hooves; besides, the horse knew every inch of the big pasture.

But it made no difference anyway, she scoffed silently. The only regret she'd have if they fell would be if the mare were injured.

She rode until she couldn't see his face anymore, until the awful words he'd said were drowned by the sound of the horse's feet against the hard ground. It took a long time, and they had covered every inch of the small acreage several times before Tracey's mind was blank enough and her senses empty enough to let her stop.

She rode slowly back to the barn and rubbed the horse down while the sun was coming up, graining both Foxfire and Trampas before she went back to the house. She staggered in across the patio, her legs numb with exhaustion, and without even trying to peel the clothes from her drained body she fell across the bed and into a desperate, dreamless sleep.

"Tracey?" Gerald's voice filtered through the line to her, as vaguely irritating as the ringing had been. "Tracey, are you all right? Has something happened to you?"

His question woke her completely, brought back

every event of the evening before with merciless precision. The last thing Gerald had said to her was that he would wait in the office!

"Gerald?" Then she stopped. She had no idea what to say next.

In the tense silence she became aware of her surroundings and of the fact that sunlight was streaming into the room. She rubbed her eyes and squinted at the bedside clock. Twelve-thirty! She hadn't come in or called on a workday!

"Well?" he demanded in an irritated voice. "What are you doing and why aren't you at work?"

"I . . . I don't know how to . . ." She couldn't finish; she couldn't put a sentence together in her head.

There was another silence, and when he spoke again his tone was entirely different. He was taking command now, and concern flowed through the wires to her.

"Tracey, stay right there. I'm coming over."

She didn't answer. Listlessly she let the buzzing receiver dangle from her hand for a few minutes, then she forced herself to hang it up. She rolled over and compelled herself to sit up, the muscles in her hips and legs screaming in protest. She hadn't ridden that long at a stretch for months.

Sleeping in her clothes hadn't helped, either, and she headed for the shower. She needed to be as together as possible when she talked to Gerald.

While she showered and dressed she thought about the decisions she'd finally reached during the endless night. She was right, she thought, knotting her wet hair onto the top of her head. She had no choice anymore.

Gerald knocked, but before going to the door she gave herself one last glance in the mirror. She pulled some tendrils loose around her face; maybe that would soften her drawn appearance.

She greeted him briefly, then led him through the house and out onto the patio. "I've just made some coffee," she said. "Would you like some?"

She turned to go back into the kitchen, but he caught her arm. "Tracey, what in the world is it? You didn't come to work, you didn't call, and now you look as if you've suffered a death in the family." His tone was both irritated and worried.

"Gerald, I can't talk about it."

"You most certainly can. I called your number all morning long. You must have been so deeply asleep that you didn't hear it, but I've called you every half hour until now I can dial your number blindfolded."

The genuine caring in his voice and the anxiety in his eyes broke down her defenses.

"Sit down, Gerald, and let me get the coffee. Then we'll talk."

While she got everything ready she thought about what to say. She might as well tell him everything at once, she decided. Get it over with.

His dark brown eyes searched her face as she settled onto the chaise longue across from his chair.

"I'm going to leave, Gerald," she said quietly, taking a sip of coffee. "I'll give you as much notice as you need to find a replacement, but sometime within the next few months I'm leaving Southwest."

"You can't!" he protested. "Tracey, you can't go."

"I can't live here anymore, Gerald. You've been wonderful to work with, and you've taught me a tremendous amount. I'll always be grateful for what you've done to help me with my career."

He was very quiet, not touching the cup on the redwood table beside him. She looked up to find his gaze boring into her. "It's Davis Turnbo, isn't it?"

Wordlessly, she nodded.

"I don't know how I figured that out," he said wryly. "Usually I'm totally dense about these things; however, this weekend I suddenly realized what was going on."

Sadly she looked at him, realizing the depth of his caring for her. She looked at the lines carved into his face beside his mouth. He had been worrying about her.

"Things aren't good between you?"

"No." The word was spoken in a tone so low she could barely hear it herself. She stared at the narrow green line that edged the top of her bisque-colored cup.

"Is that why you want to leave?"

"It's why I *have* to leave," she said, her voice slightly stronger. "I can't live the rest of my life seeing him occasionally but not being with him."

"Is there any way I can change your mind? Anything I can do?"

"No, Gerald. I wish there were, but there's nothing anyone can do."

They talked quietly while they finished their coffee; then he stood up. "I'd better get back," he said. "You try to get some rest, and don't come back to the office

until you feel better. Take a week and go someplace if
you like."

She stood, too, and began walking with him toward
his car. "No. I'll be in tomorrow, Gerald; I'm going to
work for the money to buy those rhinos. Last night,
when Davis suggested that the board give a percentage
of the money from the publicity campaign to the
preserve, I was shocked at his about-face. Now that I
think about it, I've decided that he did it because he
didn't think he was losing anything from the display
zoo—he probably doesn't expect the donations to be
enough to count."

They reached his car, and he leaned against it,
waiting for her to finish.

"There may not be," she went on, her voice hard
with determination, "but no matter what, I'm not going
to let him just *give* me anything. I'm going to work like
crazy to raise the entire amount we need. I'm going to
buy those rhinos from Fairmont before I leave Southwest."

"Great!" he responded. "Maybe by then you'll have
decided not to leave at all." He got into the car, his
movements reluctant. "I'm not going to accept your
resignation until I absolutely have to."

During the weeks that followed Tracey reaffirmed
her decision to leave Southwest. As long as she was
there she was bound to see Davis occasionally, and she
simply couldn't bear that. She was determined, though,
not to go without achieving at least one significant thing

for the preserve, and the purchase of the Fairmont rhinos was what she chose to do.

She threw herself into her work with a vengeance. She helped design a new brochure to advertise the native species exhibit. She spent long hours working with Cody and Peggy and Sand, polishing them into a charming public relations team. She made innumerable phone calls and had Lottie send letters to most of the media in the major cities of Arizona, New Mexico, Colorado, Texas and Oklahoma. Then, as they began to book appearances for her "team," she traveled with them, helping them to answer questions and make contacts.

She also began to speak to civic groups and clubs on her own again, and she attended several social functions that she would have preferred to skip just so that she could see people who might make large donations. She was going to raise enough money to buy the white rhinos from Fairmont if it took every ounce of strength in her.

She did her usual office chores at night and on weekends, and when she had to be at Southwest all day she tried to arrange it so that there was never any daylight left when she went home. She would sit in her office reading professional journals until long after everyone else had gone, or roam around the zoo checking on the animals.

But even though she worked herself into the ground and tried as hard as she could never to have a moment's leisure time, the thought of Davis was always there. For a few days after their last encounter, every time the phone rang, every time she heard a car in her drive, every time she heard footsteps in the hallway of the administration building when she was working late, she would feel an irrational thrill, a wild hope that it was he. It never was, though, and as the weeks went by she told herself that it never would be, and that the reason was that he didn't love her at all.

He would never stop loving her, he decided when a glance at his desk calendar showed him that it had been six weeks since the night he'd spent aimlessly driving the desert highways.

Wearily he leaned back in the leather desk chair and stretched his long arms, his eyes seeking the comfort of the Santa Ritas under the lowering sun. This was getting to be a habit, he thought. Most of the evenings of those weeks had found him here, trying to force his thoughts away from Tracey and onto the myriad details of business.

Tonight was worse than ever. He let his gold pen fall from his fingers onto the stack of unsigned papers and got up restlessly to walk to the long windows. The last time he'd seen her, that last kiss, those last few minutes with her in his arms, played back in his head, every detail as fresh as it had been then.

Her voice echoed in his ears, but this time its passionate intensity pulled at him as strongly as the hurt usually did. He let all the words of love she had spoken spread through him in rhythm with the beating of his heart; then he turned abruptly away from the brilliant orange and purple sky and strode across the dark room. He dialed the phone, then listened as it rang for an endless time. There was never any answer.

Tracey signed the last of the thank-you letters to recent contributors and tossed them into her out basket. The offices seemed cavernously empty—Gerald was out of town, Lottie was already gone, and no one else seemed to be in the building.

She glanced at her watch. Only three o'clock. She really should stay at least another hour; there might be some calls about the arrangements for Dehli.

But she had to have something to do; she had to have movement. She paced to the window, but the sight of the paths full of visitors didn't soothe her. Their entry fees wouldn't be going to her special fund, and although all her work with the publicity campaign had raised more than half the money she needed to buy the Fairmont rhinos, time was running out.

Nervously she tightened the belt of her dress and tried to think of other ways to generate donations. If only there was something exciting happening at the preserve, something that would earn some new publicity, new publicity in which she could make an appeal for donations. If she didn't get enough contributions to buy those rhinos, she would leave Southwest feeling as if she was a failure.

The ringing of her phone interrupted her thoughts. It was probably the airline again about the connections in Singapore. She went back to her desk and took the receiver from the cradle. "Tracey Johnston."

"Tracey."

The one word shattered her. His voice was rich and sexy, and the confident way he said her name sent pleasure shimmering through her body. She could see him; she could feel him. It was as if all the distance and the time between them had telescoped into nothingness in the one second it had taken for him to speak her name.

She held the phone to her ear with a feverish grip, and as his voice went on she let the sound of it flow over her taut nerves in a tonal caress. Then it stopped, and she realized that he was waiting for an answer. She hadn't heard the question; in fact, she hadn't heard a single individual word since he'd spoken her name.

"Tracey, are you there?"

"Yes," she managed at last. "I'm sorry, Davis, would you repeat that?"

"I said, don't despair if you don't have enough money yet to buy your rhinos. I've found something for the preserve."

This time the words reached her. "What is it?"

"A cougar. One of the men on my ranch found a fresh kill this morning. If the cat beds down close to it tonight, he might still be in the area tomorrow."

"And you're going to hunt him?" she asked a little unsteadily. Just listening to him was enough to devastate her.

"Yes. Since the kill was one of my cows, I want to get rid of him. Why don't you bring Doc Reed and his stun gun over early in the morning? Bring your camera, too, and get some pictures to publicize your native species exhibit."

Go over there? Actually see Davis after she'd spent all this time trying to wipe out every memory of him?

"Davis, I . . ." She had to think of some excuse. If he could do *this* to her just over the phone . . . "I could send a photographer."

"No. There'll be too many people involved as it is. We can't take half of Tucson on a cat hunt." He waited, silent.

He was right, she thought, her mind and pulse both racing. She could use this to create the extra publicity she had to have if she was going to get the rest of the money for the rhinos. "All right," she said finally. "I'll make the arrangements."

"Meet me at the Highway 86 gate to the ranch. I'll be there at sun-up."

"We'll be there," she promised, and with a quick good-bye she hung up the phone.

She dropped her head into her hands, and with a gesture that was fast becoming habitual ran her fingers into her hair to massage her aching temples. Just hearing his voice had made it so much worse. It had aroused her whole body; now she was throbbing with the longing to be with him.

Then the devastating pain of loss obliterated the desire. He hadn't had one personal word to say. He'd given no indication that they'd ever been more than business acquaintances.

How could he have forgotten? How could he throw away that wild passion that beat in their veins when they were together, that galvanic sensuality that pulsed in the air between them?

She raised her head and shook the hair back from her face, determinedly reaching for the phone to call Dr. Reed. She'd see Davis, but she wouldn't give those wild passions a chance to flare again, to draw her back into the morass of misery that she'd just begun to fight her way out of. If he could forget, so could she.

Chapter Thirteen

Davis left the house long before daybreak. He drove the familiar stretches of highway without consciously thinking of what he was doing, following the beams of the headlights as they pierced the predawn darkness. When he reached the narrow road that led to this remote section of his holdings he pulled off and parked to wait for the truck from Southwest to arrive.

His long body relaxed behind the wheel, but his nerves were taut as they had been all night; unconsciously he drummed his fingers against the wheel. He stared out into the blackness, not caring that with the lights of the truck extinguished he saw nothing at all. Nothing except Tracey's passionate face as she cried out to him, "I want forever with you." The memory knifed at him, and he jerked open the door and stepped out into the chilly air.

The sun was streaking the sky in the east when he saw them approaching at last—a longbed pickup truck of the dark green color that was standard for the zoo and preserve, a cage lashed onto the back of it. His eyes went to the cab as if drawn by a magnetic force, and once they found the glint of Tracey's fiery hair in the pale light they clung to it as if it were a beacon.

She saw him even before they turned off the highway. Her pulse stopped, then began to beat again erratically. He was leaning against the hood of his truck, his booted feet crossed, a western-style hat pulled low over his face. Thirstily she drank in the sight of him; her eyes roamed over his muscular thighs encased in tight faded jeans, his slim waist under the wide belt, his broad chest beneath the woven cotton shirt.

"Looks like we've found it," she said inanely, tearing her eyes away from Davis to look at Dr. Reed instead.

"Right," he agreed sleepily.

Davis was at her window almost before she'd stopped the truck. "Move over," he said. "Jim'll follow us from his cabin with the dogs, and we'll all drive as far as we can up toward where he found the kill."

"I can drive," she replied coolly.

"I'll drive." His tone was flatly sure, and he opened her door as he spoke, so rather than make a scene in front of Dr. Reed, she moved over to make room for him.

His thigh touched hers as he slid onto the seat, and as

he settled in and took the wheel it rested solidly against hers from hip to knee. Heat flooded through her entire body at the contact.

With a quick movement she tried to put some space between them, but there wasn't room enough.

He shifted the gears and started up the narrow road. Then he looked down into her eyes with a sideways glance, his blue gaze piercing her, his smile an enticement.

"Hi, Tracey."

She couldn't move her head, couldn't break the look. She ran her tongue over her lips. "Hello," she said at last.

"How're you, Doc?" he asked, looking across her to the veterinarian. "This too early for you?"

"It seems to be," Dr. Reed said ruefully. "I'm just not used to it anymore. Why, when I was a boy . . ."

As he went on to expound on the virtues of early rising Tracey floated in the world of overpowering sensations that only Davis could bring into being. The pressure of his leg against hers increased ever so slightly as he drove them up into the hills, and both the conversation in the truck and the countryside outside its windows faded away in the luxury of being near him. Being this close made every nerve in her body yearn toward his.

She glanced up at his face, wishing that her fingers could trace the sensual shape of his mouth under the blond mustache, remembering the taste of it against her own. Her throat tightened around the hard knot of tears that was forming there. Even if they touched each other again, if they made love, it would be for just one more time.. He didn't love her enough to stay with her.

Abruptly she ran one hand through her thick hair and turned her head to stare unseeingly out the windshield at the breathtaking beauty of the mountains. Why had she done this to herself? Why had she come?

She said very little as they stopped briefly at Jim's cabin. He was waiting by his truck, the dogs in a box in the back, and he pulled out ahead of them to take the lead up the narrowing road. Dr. Reed and Davis discussed tranquilizing the cougar, and Davis told them a story of one of Jim's cougar hunting trips to Utah. After what seemed to her to be hours of driving up what had become a mere track, Jim stopped and Davis pulled up behind him.

Davis got out, and so did Dr. Reed, but she remained sitting for a moment, irrationally resenting the few yards of distance that were between them. She felt naked now without his leg against hers.

Disgusted with herself, she reached for her camera. She was losing her mind. It was a mistake to have seen him at all, and the farther apart they were, the better. Well, at least she'd made the right decision about leaving Southwest, she thought resignedly as she began getting out of the truck. She couldn't take much more of this.

Dimly she was aware that Jim had let the dogs out of the box, and that they were snuffling around the place where the cat had been the day before. One of them let out a long, throaty howl, and the other two began to bark loudly.

"I think it's a big lion," Jim shouted over the din. "We'll have him by dark if we're lucky."

By dark! Would she have to endure a whole day of this torture? She couldn't stand being with Davis that long unless she was in his arms.

The hounds were already out of sight. "Aren't we going to follow them?" she asked.

"Not yet," Davis said. "We're going to let them line out on the track. There's a good chance the cat circled and crossed this road up ahead."

"Have some coffee," Jim said, offering her a paper cup full of the hot liquid he'd just poured from his thermos.

She took it gratefully and walked a few feet away from them to stare out across the serrated peaks of the Santa Ritas. She could feel Davis's eyes on her, but she didn't even glance at him. Instead she held herself tautly aloof and sipped the coffee, her face turned away from him.

The sun on her back was getting hotter by the minute, and she felt almost dizzy. She'd slept very little the previous night, caught in the hopeless tug of war between dread of and anticipation at being with him, and now she cursed herself for having come. She could have left this to Davis and Dr. Reed and forgotten all about the stupid photographs. Nothing, not even her precious rhinos, was worth this anguish.

"Here they come," Jim called then, and she turned to see the dogs cross the road right in front of Jim's truck, just as Davis had predicted.

"They're headed for Grayson's Canyon," Davis said. "Let's go."

He came rapidly across the road and took her arm, but as they started into the scrubby brush beside the road she pulled away from his touch.

He gave no sign that he'd noticed. "Good thing you wore your boots," he remarked, glancing down at her feet. "This may be quite a hike."

"I hope not," she said shortly. "I've got a lot of other things to do today."

Dr. Reed and Jim went on ahead, moving very fast, but Davis walked more slowly beside her, as self-assured as if he belonged there. Frustration edged along her spine. "What are you doing with that?" she asked irritably, gesturing toward the rifle he'd taken from Jim's truck.

"I only brought it in case Dr. Reed should miss and the cat should jump," he said soothingly. "Don't worry, I won't kill your cougar unless he attacks."

The real concern for her and for her feelings about the animal that she heard in his voice penetrated her exasperation, and she felt vaguely ashamed of speaking to him so sharply. She sighed. Darn it! She just couldn't win.

Her thoughts were interrupted by a shout up ahead. Both Jim and Dr. Reed were waving to them furiously, and the dogs were barking nonstop.

"Come on," Davis said, taking her arm again, this time in a grip that said he wouldn't let go. "You're about to see your first cougar in the wild."

They climbed over and around some large rocks and went through scattered piñons and junipers to the spot where Jim and Dr. Reed were standing. The veterinarian was already loading his gun, and Jim was watching his dogs howling and barking, jumping all over each other at the foot of a small tree.

The cat was sitting in the tree, staring at all of them with a fierce, feline intensity. A thrill raced through Tracey, the same magnificent excitement that had riveted her to the deck of the boat when they'd seen the bighorn sheep. Davis was completely still beside her, and without even looking at him she knew that he was feeling that same joyous exhilaration. They were caught up again in a marvelous shared moment.

Everything was frozen for a long instant. Nobody moved or spoke. The cat was the stillest of all. Only the noise of the dogs broke the mountain quiet.

"It's always seemed odd to me that a cat will generally run or climb a tree instead of fighting the dogs," Jim said. "He could kill them all with one slap of his paw."

His words broke the crystalline moment, and instinctively Tracey raised her camera to record what was happening. The splendid animal still didn't move; the tawny litheness of its body seemed glued to the gnarled branch of the tree. She snapped the shutter again and again, the cougar's defiant face filling her vision. Then she lowered the camera.

Dr. Reed took aim, and the dart went home, deep into the neck of the cat. Before it fell from the tree Jim was putting the leashes on his dogs, pulling them away from the site, though they were obviously reluctant to leave.

Davis and Jim went back to the truck to take the dogs and get the cage for the cougar, while she and Dr. Reed stayed with the big cat. She crouched down beside it, running her hand over the gorgeous pelt.

"Isn't he glorious?" she asked. "It's hard to believe that he's real."

"Oh, he's real all right," the doctor replied with a chuckle. "And if I misjudged his dosage we could find that out in a hurry."

He monitored the cougar's breathing, and when the others returned he helped move it into the cage for the trip to the preserve. The three men carried the cage easily, and Tracey followed, the invigoration of the experience still strumming in her veins as they arrived at the road again.

They slid the caged cat onto the Southwest truck. With a start she noticed that the box of dogs was beside it instead of on Jim's truck.

Davis turned to see the direction of her gaze. "I asked Jim to leave his truck for us," he said.

She stared at him. "For us? What do you mean?"

Suddenly all the old sexual tension and all the pain of the weeks they'd spent apart hung in the air between them.

"While you're here with your camera you'll want to get some shots of Mt. Wrightson," he said smoothly. "It's a real favorite of photographers."

He took a few steps toward her, his eyes gleaming from beneath the brim of his hat. His tone was low and sexy, and both it and his eyes told her plainly that photographing mountains was the last thing on his mind.

She played with the camera strap around her neck, her fingers shaking a little. Her mind was shouting that she should insist on going back to the preserve with Dr. Reed, that she should rush back to the refuge of her office and immerse herself in work, that she should busy herself shoring up the wall she'd been erecting between them for the past weeks.

But her treacherous body annihilated that logic. It was clamoring to feel every inch of his against it, and without any conscious volition she took a step toward him, drowning in the depths of his eyes.

"All right," she said at last. Her breathing was so shallow that her voice was barely audible. She tried again. "That sounds like a good idea," she said more loudly, and forced herself to walk past him to the truck, where she told Dr. Reed and Jim good-bye.

As the others drove away he turned to her. "Now you know that this whole cougar hunt was nothing but an excuse to get you up into the mountains with me," he said. "The entire thing was staged."

In spite of the heady mixture of emotions that were rushing through her, she laughed. "Well, you certainly did a good job of directing—you got an especially good performance from the cat."

"I thought so," he replied with his teasing grin. "In fact, his behavior was so natural and he seemed so at home in the wild that it reminded me of the day we saw the bighorn sheep." His tone was heavy with meaning, the probing look in his eyes both a question and a statement.

Quickly she looked away, and when she did he reached for her hand. "Come on," he said softly. "There really is a spot I want you to see."

His hand holding hers was a catalyst for her senses. It made the high mountain air fresher than it had been, the scent of the pines sharper and the calls of the birds clearer than they had been only seconds before. He walked a little ahead of her to show the way, but he never let go of her hand.

They walked in silence for a hundred yards or so, and then he led her through a sparse stand of Ponderosa pines onto a promontory overlooking the wide sweep of the Santa Rita range.

She absorbed the sight with all her senses. The broad sweep of open spaces, the meeting of earth and sky, the morning sun highlighting the majestic, serrated peaks moved her almost to tears. "Oh, Davis, it's miraculous," she breathed at last. "It's absolutely splendid."

He looked down at her, the glow in her eyes reflected in his smile. "And so are you," he murmured huskily. "So are you."

He let go of her hand for the first time and raised his own to feather his fingers against her cheek. Then, as if that one ephemeral touch had set free all the pent-up longing in his soul, he reached for her. He pulled her against him with both arms, a ragged moan coming from deep within him.

He rained kisses on her hair; then his warm lips pushed its heavy mass away from her face and neck to find and fondle the sensitive lobe of her ear and the nape of her neck.

With a shattering sigh she let her thin defenses crumble and fell back across his arm, giving herself up to the exquisite sensations that he was arousing in her. She was completely a creature of feeling now; thoughts and doubts had nothing at all to do with her at this moment. Davis was her only actuality; his lips and his tongue, the faint prickle of his mustache against her skin, were her only awareness of being alive.

His lips found hers and caressed them lightly, then held them gently still to meet the sensitizing tip of his tongue. Her lips fell apart for his explorations, and he stroked every inch of her mouth with his tongue while his hands demanded that she let them do the same to her body.

"Oh, Tracey, I love you," he said at last. His hands on her shoulders pushed her away just enough so that he could see into her eyes while he held their lower bodies in intimate contact.

Bitter tears came swiftly to quiver on her lashes as she looked up at him, his words reverberating in her ears. Next he would say that they could always remember this beautiful day together. It could be one of their one days at a time!

Fiercely she twisted away, able to jerk herself from his grasp because of the suddenness of her movement. "Don't say that to me!" she cried, almost choking on the words. "I don't want to hear it again."

She turned to go, but he grabbed both her hands with

a quick gesture and pulled her down to the bed of pine needles scattered under the trees.

"Sit down," he commanded, his voice shaking in its intensity. "Listen to me."

He still held both her hands, and she stopped trying to pull away.

"I've been thinking about nothing but you for weeks," he told her, his penetrating eyes pinning hers. "I went over and over what you said to me the last time I saw you, and at first all I could think of was what you said about not wanting to see me again. I remembered that because I thought it was what I deserved to hear. If I couldn't make a commitment, then I had no right to get involved with you."

His look assaulted her, ripped at her; he was trying to see into her head. Her mind reeled with the force of it; his eyes were on a level with hers as they sat on the rough ground, his face just inches away. She couldn't think at all for the love and desire and pain mixing in her veins, so his last few words were the only ones she took in.

When she'd absorbed them, her heart dropped. He hadn't brought her up here to look at the mountains; he'd brought her here to tell her good-bye!

She pulled, trying to get away from him, but he wouldn't let go of her hands.

"No. Let me finish. Tracey, darling, I love you so much, and I knew that if you weren't happy with me, I couldn't live."

The endearment and the throbbing poignance in his

voice stopped her struggle. All the fury went out of her, and confusion took its place.

He really did love her. It was there, unmistakably there in his face, in his eyes, in his voice. So why was he telling her good-bye?

Suddenly she found it too frustrating to try to figure it out, to try to think at all. She *wouldn't* think about it now. It hurt too much. She'd been suffering for eons, and his arms around her and his lips on hers just now had given her the only release she'd had. She wanted that total escape from reality one more time before the pain came back to stay.

She leaned toward him, balanced precariously on her knees on the incline slightly above him, and he pulled her to him, shifting them around to lean into the twisting trunk of the tree. Her body fit into the curve of his, and his warmth implanted every cell in her body with fertile seeds of desire.

"Tracey, have you? . . ."

Slowly she moved around, turning to lean back against his raised knee so she could see his face. With one hand she gently took off his hat, and with the other she touched his lips. She lifted her face to his; then, before her lips touched his mouth, she threaded her fingers through his hair and traced the line where the hat band had been. "Kiss me," she murmured huskily. "Don't talk to me, Davis. Kiss me."

He groaned and took her mouth with his, drawing the nectar from it with skillful thrusts of his tongue until she was limp with longing. His hands held her away from him instead of to him, but they roamed over her shoulders, her back, the curve of her waist, with the prideful leisure of possession. Then, although he found her breast and cupped it warmly, he broke the kiss.

She whimpered in protest and, her eyes still closed, threw her arms around his neck. "Again," she murmured into his ear, loving the feathering of his breath against her neck, craving the magical escape for one more infinite moment.

His chuckle was rich and loving. "In a minute," he said. "I want to finish what I was saying when I was so rudely interrupted."

She tried to close her ears. "No," she whispered.

"Yes, I want to tell you." He gently stroked her back. "While I've been doing all this thinking about you, I've been wondering if you've raised enough money yet to buy your rhinos from Fairmont."

Shocked by the unexpected words, she pulled away from him and stared into his eyes. The expression in them was quizzical, mysterious, loving, inquiring—so many things that she couldn't sort them all out. She tried to answer, but her mind refused to consider such a mundane topic.

"Well?" he prodded.

Finally she answered. "No. I lack about five thousand dollars."

He raised one eyebrow and slowly traced a circle on her shoulder blade. "Not bad. You'll probably get them, then."

"I doubt it. Time's running out, and the contributions have slowed down to a trickle."

"Well, maybe someone will give the whole amount to you as a personal gift," he said lightly.

Irritated with his sudden change of subject and manner, sick with being forced to come back into the real world, she sat up straighter and looked out across the mountains. "I see no hope of that," she said flatly. "There's no occasion for anyone to be giving me a gift."

"I think a wedding is an occasion," he drawled. "And it's customary for the groom to give the bride a wedding gift. Would you accept three rather cantankerous pachyderms donated to Southwest Wild Animal Preserve in the name of Tracey Turnbo?"

Her eyes flew back to him and searched his face. The love and the hope that she saw etched into every line of it brought her heart pounding into her throat.

"Tracey Turnbo?" she repeated with trembling lips. "Marriage? But Davis, you don't want to be committed. . . ."

"I *didn't* want to be committed to anyone," he corrected gently. "But ever since I finally heard something else you told me that night after the board meeting, I've decided that being committed to you is *all* I want."

"What did I tell you?"

"That you wanted forever with me."

The words hung between them in the quiet morning air.

"That was exactly what I was feeling for you, too, but my guilt about the past wouldn't let me see it. I knew I wanted you and loved you, but I kept thinking that if I made a commitment to you, I'd be taking a chance on ruining your happiness forever."

"But, Davis, *you* didn't ruin Marla's happiness. . . ."

"Probably not. I've spent hours and hours thinking about that since we talked that night at the lake. You were right; she'd had problems before we were married. I knew that, but I thought I'd be able to solve them." He smiled ruefully. "I guess I always try to take too much responsibility for everybody else. I have ever since I was a little kid worrying about whether or not my father was going to lose our ranch."

She smiled at him tenderly. "Sometimes that's a really sweet trait," she told him. "Trying to take care of everybody."

"And sometimes it gets me in a whole lot of trouble," he answered. He brushed his lips across her forehead. "I've just been so scared because you're such a dreamer," he murmured. "And I wish I could make every one of your dreams come true. I wish that besides the rhinos I could give you your grotto for the snow leopards and a whole herd of every species you could ever want for the preserve and . . ."

"The way I feel right now, I don't care where the snow leopards live," she told him, the teasing light of love shining in her eyes. "All I care about is that *I* get to live with *you.*"

His questioning glance searched her face. "Tracey, do you think you really can live with an ornery old realist like me?"

"I know I can," she told him solemnly Then the

teasing smile lit her eyes again. "In fact, I'm going to go right to work and try to make a bit of a dreamer of you, too."

The smile that her words brought to his lips held all the wonder of the love he had for her. "You've already done that, my darling," he whispered. "You've already done that."

She just looked at him, completely overcome by the miracle of their love.

He voiced her thought, carefully spacing the momentous words. "And all I know is that if we both have the exact same dream, then we'd be fools not to try to make it come true."

His movements rough in his earnestness, he took her head in both his hands. "I know you meant that the night you said it, Tracey . . . about wanting me forever." His eyes clouded as he paused. "But after all this time . . . all this pain . . . can you say it now and still mean it?"

She looked back at him with her soul in her eyes. "I want you forever. I mean it," she vowed solemnly.

Joy flared in his face, and he sat very still for a long, long moment, loving her with his eyes.

Then she added with an impish grin, "And I also meant it a few minutes ago when I asked you to kiss me!"

"Well, that's something you'll never have to ask for again," he growled, and he took her lips with his.

Silhouette Desire

APRIL TITLES

NIGHTWALKER
Stephanie James

TAKE ALL MYSELF
Lucy Gordon

TOO NEAR THE FIRE
Lindsay McKenna

AFFAIRS OF STATE
Sara Fitzgerald

TIMELESS RITUALS
Laurel Evans

RARE BREED
Janet Joyce

Four New Silhouette Romances could be yours

ABSOLUTELY FREE

Did you know that Silhouette Romances are no longer available from the shops in the U.K?

Read on to discover how you could receive four brand new Silhouette Romances, **free** and **without obligation,** with this special introductory offer to the new Silhouette Reader Service.

As thousands of women who have read these books know — Silhouette Romances sweep you away into an exciting love filled world of fascination between men and women. A world filled with

age-old conflicts — love and money, ambition and guilt, jealousy and pride, even life and death.

Silhouette Romances are the latest stories written by the world's best romance writers, and they are **only** available from Silhouette Reader Service. Take out a subscription and you could receive 6 brand new titles every month, plus a newsletter bringing you all the latest information from Silhouette's New York editors. All this delivered in one exciting parcel direct to your door, with no charges for postage and packing.

And at only 95p for a book, Silhouette Romances represent the very best value in Romantic Reading.

Remember, Silhouette Romances are **only** available to subscribers, so don't miss out on this very special opportunity. Fill in the certificate below and post it today. You don't even need a stamp.

--- ✂ ---

FREE BOOK CERTIFICATE

To: Silhouette Reader Service, FREEPOST, P.O. Box 236, Croydon, Surrey. CR9 9EL

Yes, please send me, free and without obligation, four brand new Silhouette Romances and reserve a subscription for me. If I decide to subscribe, I shall receive six brand new books every month for £5.70*, post and packing free. If I decide not to subscribe I shall write to you within 10 days. The free books are mine to keep, whatever I decide. I understand that I may cancel my subscription at any time simply by writing to you. I am over 18 years of age. Please write in BLOCK CAPITALS.

Signature _____

Name _____

Address _____

_____ Postcode _____

SEND NO MONEY — TAKE NO RISKS.
Please don't forget to include your Postcode.

*Remember postcodes speed delivery. Offer applies in U.K. only and is not valid to present subscribers. Silhouette reserve the right to exercise discretion in granting membership. If price changes are necessary you will be notified. Offer expires July 1985. *Subject to possible VAT*

EPS1

Silhouette Special Edition

APRIL TITLES

OPPOSITES ATTRACT
Nora Roberts

SEA OF DREAMS
Angel Milan

WILD PASSIONS
Gena Dalton

PROMISES TO KEEP
Carolyn Thornton

DANGEROUS COMPANY
Laura Parker

SOMEDAY SOON
Kathleen Eagle